ALSO BY LAURA KASISCHKE

WILD BRIDES
HOUSEKEEPING IN A DREAM
SUSPICIOUS RIVER

WHITE
BIRD
IN
A
BLIZZARD

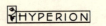

NEW YORK

WHITE BIRD IN A BLIZZARD

LAURA KASISCHKE

Library of Congress Cataloging-in-Publication Data
Kasischke, Laura.
White bird in a blizzard / Laura Kasischke. — 1st ed.
p.   cm.
ISBN 0-7868-6366-8
I. Title.
PS3561.A6993W53   1998
813'.54—dc21   98-11223
CIP

Book design by Holly McNeely

FIRST EDITION

10   9   8   7   6   5   4   3   2   1

for Bill

I WOULD LIKE TO THANK
BILL ABERNETHY, LISA BANKOFF,
JENNIFER BARTH AND ANTONYA NELSON
FOR HELPING ME WRITE
AND REWRITE THIS NOVEL;
ED AND JUNE KASISCHKE
FOR MANY YEARS OF ENCOURAGEMENT;
AND LUCY AND JACK ABERNETHY,
MY CHILDREN, FOR LOVE.

WHITE BIRD

IN A BLIZZARD

ONE

JANUARY 1986

I AM SIXTEEN WHEN MY MOTHER STEPS OUT OF HER SKIN ONE frozen January afternoon—pure self, atoms twinkling like microscopic diamond chips around her, perhaps the chiming of a clock, or a few bright flute notes in the distance—and disappears.

No one sees her leave, but she is gone.

Only the morning before, my mother was a housewife—a housewife who, for twenty years, kept our house as swept up and sterile as the mind of winter itself, so perhaps she finally just whisk-broomed herself out, a luminous cloud of her drifting through the bedroom window as soft as talcum powder, mingling with the snowflakes as they fell, and the stardust and the lunar ash out there.

Her name is Eve, and this is Garden Heights, Ohio, so I used to like to think of my mother as Eve—the naked one, the first one—when she was in the Garden, poisoning the weeds with bleach, defoliating the trees, stuffing their leaves down the garbage disposal, then scouring the sink with something chemical and harsh, but powdered, something dyed ocean blue to disguise its deadly powers for the housewives like my mother who bought it, only dimly realizing that what they'd purchased with its snappy name (Spic and Span, Mr. Clean, Fantastik) was pure acid.

The blue of a child's eyes, the blue of a robin's egg—

But swallow a teaspoon of that and it will turn your intestines to lace.

This Eve, like the first one, was bored in Garden Heights. She spent her afternoons in the silence of a house she'd just cleaned yesterday from bottom to top, and there was nothing left for her to do beyond planning the nothing of the future, too.

Sometimes, when I came home from school early, I'd find her asleep in my bed. She'd be dressed as if she had somewhere to go—black slacks, a lamb's-wool sweater, pearls, dark hair set in smooth curls—folded onto her side, not a single light on in the whole house. But that afternoon, something else happened.

What, I can only imagine.

I imagine her standing at the bedroom window watching the sky toss its cold litter of snow on the lawn, thinking about loss, or love, or lust, bored again, then exploding like a bomb of feather-duster feathers, or melting into the wall to wall—a milky, evaporating shadow on the shag.

When my father gets home from work, she is gone completely. When I get home from school, he is sitting in the living room with his suit still on, hands turned up empty on his lap.

We wait all night for her to come home, but she doesn't.

We don't eat dinner. We don't know how.

My sheets feel frozen when I get in bed, and I can hear my father snoring in their bedroom.

I realize now that I knew nothing about my mother except that one day she was here—making dinner, cleaning the house, scowling around with that feather duster—and the next day she wasn't.

BUT WHAT COULD I HAVE DONE ABOUT MY MOTHER? WHILE she was metamorphosing right in our own home—changing, reshaping, going crazy, or sane—I was becoming sixteen. I thought her trouble was just menopause, or boredom, and by the time I might have said or done something, I *was* sixteen, my blood like a little creek flooded suddenly with hormones, a babbling brook that had become hot, and high, and dangerous.

I fell in love with the boy next door, and my own flesh became a thing I'd never really worn before. Sometimes, pressing my palms together, I thought I felt a magnetic field between them—something invisible but shaped, like sound, or heat, an egg of light—and it was as though I could hold the life force itself in my hands.

Whatever my mother was up to, I didn't care.

Phil, the boy next door, is tall, and blond, and actively stupid. "Fuckin' A," he'll say when a bit of poetry is quoted by the TV news anchor. "Straight C's!" he smiles, waving his report card at me in the cafeteria at school.

In the summer, he wanted me to wear nothing but halter tops, and when we met in our backyards, which were separated only by a yellow ditch of daffodils, he'd come up behind me and slip his hands into the top.

The fertilized lawns throbbed like green glass in the sun.

"Show me," I would say to Phil as he drove us to school in his father's sedan, and he'd unzip his pants, take his penis out, flop it around.

———

Phil has been my boyfriend for a year, and in that year we have talked about almost nothing. If he has any original ideas, any personal opinions wafting around like feathers in his head, he manages to keep them mostly to himself. He listens to WKLL, the heaviest of the heavy-metal stations around here, but he's not the heavy-metal type. He's never been to a concert, and can't remember the names of the bands he likes or tell you what his favorite song of the month is called, let alone what it's about, all that car-crash clutter behind the singing.

He's what you'd call a clean-cut kid if you were the type of person who believed in clean-cut kids. No ripped T-shirts. No tattoos. No steel-tipped boots. As suburban as it gets.

But it's always in the background as he's driving, and he nods his head as if he's listening ("W-*KILL!*" the disc jockeys scream between songs, sounding juvenile and half-hearted and nonviolent), as if he's enjoying what he hears, as if it speaks to some part of him that is not the least bit visible to the naked eye, some slam-dancing protozoan part.

I've learned to tune it out, myself, having always worried that if I listened, really listened, to that kind of music, it might fry some delicate tissue in my inner ear and I'd go deaf.

Phil doesn't talk much, but it doesn't matter. If I'd wanted to talk, I could have talked to my mother. For a long time, she was trying to get me to talk—

"Kat," she said, "do you love this boy?"

"*Mom,*" I said, turning on her. "What business is that of yours?"

She was standing behind me in the bathroom, looking over my shoulder at the two of us reflected in the mirror above the sink. Just out of the shower, I had a towel wrapped around me, and a veil of steam came between us

and smudged our reflections. The humidity smoothed the
lines out on her face, and she looked like a foggy me.

"Well, I can't stand your father," she said then, and
the bluntness of it was like a rubber bat slugging into a
rubber ball.

"Jesus Christ," I said. "Tell it to someone else," and
pushed past her into the hall.

As simply as my mother was here, and then she wasn't,
Phil and I were virgins, and then we weren't.

One afternoon when we had no school—my father
was at work, my mother was still at the mall—we got into
my bed, which was decorated with pansies and piled with
stuffed animals that I knocked in one smooth gesture to
the floor while Phil stood behind me, thumbs hooked into
belt loops, waiting.

Phil is lanky, and when he stands in one place he rests
all his weight on one leg, and this turns his body into nothing but angles and planes, a boy made of scrap metal.

It was March, and the light that bled in under the
window shades was blurred and pale, as if March had gray
water in her veins.

We undid each other's buttons and zippers under the
covers. Neither of us said a word. We stomped our clothes
down to the bottom of the bed in a panic of embarrassment
and desire, a kind of prone peasant dancing—trampling the
grapes, mashing the potatoes. I rolled onto my back, and
wondered what I would know next that I'd never known
before. Sin? Ecstasy? My own mortality? A glimpse of the
cosmos as he entered me?

But when Phil rolled on top of me, what I had was a
sudden knowledge of skin.

How much of it there is.

How, like an elastic sock, it's slipped over all the mystery and liquid that make us live. I could feel Phil's heart

thumping in it, bobbing like a plastic boat in a warm and salty bath, and I could hear that ocean, too, sloshing between his lungs. When he started going faster, getting ready to come, rocking the bed, turning red, he pushed my thighs farther apart with his arms, grimaced horrifically, and the two of us sounded like wet rags being furiously slapped together—

If it hadn't been for skin, we would have spilled.

So, this was what was on my mind that spring and summer and fall into the bitter beginning of this winter—taking up all my time, occupying all my thoughts—as my mother was preparing herself to vanish, buying miniskirts and birds, talking to herself in the kitchen, hissing at me as I passed her in the hall, making confessions I didn't want to hear. Just as my mother's body was turning to glass, cracking all along the spine. Just as my mother was about to become nothing but invisible particles of brightness and air, I was becoming nothing *but* my body.

Even in the middle of U.S. History, I could smell myself—blood and semen and spit and sweat—between my legs. I'd see him turn a corner in the hallway of our high school, and I would nearly groan with it, imagining the arc of him—hairless and hard, and all that skin—over me in my bed. I'd close my eyes in Psychology and picture my own legs spread, seeing myself from the sky, my nipples pointed up at me, and that teary pinkness waiting for Phil, or God, or something to fill it up.

Desiring him had made me suddenly desire everything. Some nights I'd dream I was lying on a table in a restaurant—maybe Bob's Chop House—naked, a sprig of parsley near my feet, maybe even an apple in my mouth, and every boy at my high school, maybe even the men—the principal, the janitors, all of them—were lined up, all of them with hard-ons, looking at me hungrily, with Phil at the end of the line, the longest and hardest and hungriest of them all.

This was a whole new planet I suddenly found myself living on, wading every day through a sexual river on fire, and the last thing on my mind was my mother—who was slipping out of the physical world just as I slipped in.

THE FIRST NIGHT MY MOTHER'S GONE I DREAM MY SHEETS have turned to snow, and their cold white wraps me in winter like a stillborn baby. The light, the bed, the sheets—it's as if a pale angel, enormous, is kneeling over me, a colossus of pure marble, as if she is pressing me with her bare-fingered wings back into the womb of January in Ohio—

I am the small o slipping into the other O, the large empty O that swallows everything whole.

Maybe it would be sweet there, but I'm not ready to go.

The walls begin to throb—electric, frozen. They are frost-furred, and contracting. I realize that if I can't swim to the surface, these walls will embrace me to death—inevitably, but with affection. I struggle for a long time against them.

When I wake up, my father's sitting at the edge of my bed.

"That was your mother who called," he says, though I haven't heard the phone ring. "She said she's never coming back."

I raise myself up on my elbows, "What?"

I ask it without expression.

He doesn't answer.

He hides his face in his hands. "Oh, Kat," he sobs, "what are we going to do?"

SHE NAMED ME KATRINA BECAUSE SHE WANTED TO CALL ME Kat. She wanted to call me Kat because I was to be her pet. "Here, Kat. Here, kitty kitty kitty," she'd call, and I'd come. Sometimes she'd even pat my head, scratch behind my ears.

Katrina. A kind of fancy cat. A Russian breed, perhaps. The kind of cat that decorates the couch just by sleeping on it.

So, for a while I thought I *was* my mother's pet, and nothing but. When I got old enough to get the joke, I'd even purr for her, crawl to wherever she was sitting and rub against her legs.

But when I got even older, I'd glare at her in silence when she called me, and stand my ground. She'd hiss through her teeth, swat in my direction with her claws, and laugh. After a while, I couldn't stand her. The sound of her crossing the living room in slippers made my head ache. And after I fell in love with Phil, just as I wanted less of her, she wanted more and more of me. I would sit across the kitchen table from her in the morning while she drank coffee and stared at me, and I thought, If I look up, this woman will swallow me whole.

But I was her pet for a long time, despite how quickly the time went by. I remember the sound of her voice, naming everything, when I still knew the names for nothing. *Woof*, she said, pointing at the neighbor's dog scratching in our garden. It was big and blond, fur like polished straw, and wore a collar with tags that made silvery music under our kitchen window. It dug and dug. "Let it," my mother said, even though it was ruining her petunias. "Let it figure out for itself there's nothing there."

Snake, she said as she held me up to the terrarium at the back of the pet store where the air smelled of piss and vinegar and wood chips. The snake was asleep, coiled and breathing, like my father's garden hose in the garage. I remember there were smudged fingerprints on the glass— round, human designs, perfectly reproduced, lines spiraling into tiny, receding eyes—as if someone had wanted to leave some evidence behind.

Bird, she said as we were walking out of the pet store and one smashed itself against the bars of its cage in our direction—a pretty fist, white and screeching, something an old lady might wear on her hat to church on Sunday.

And I remember lying beside her in my parents' bed one morning after my father had gone to work.

Frost had scribbled the windows, but I couldn't read what it said. I couldn't read at all yet. Whenever my mother opened a book, I had to trust that the story she told me was the one that was written there. And later, of course, when I could read, I'd find out that, more often than not, it wasn't.

My mother had a sense of humor.

For instance, at the end of "Rumpelstiltskin," the queen does not have to give her baby up to the manic, miniature man who demands it. The reason she's wearing that beatific cookie-cutter smile is because she's tricked him, learned his name, and gets to keep her firstborn, not because she's just given the baby away.

She has black hair.

We are laughing.

It is a nest of feathered pillows here, both of us in white gowns. Silly, she pulls the bedsheet over our heads, and with the morning light streaming in, the sheet is a whole heaven above us, blinding me with brightness, and for a moment I've lost her in it. "*Mama*," I call, and the syllables rise from my mouth like small and cold balloons.

"Kat," she says, "here's Mama," from somewhere beside me inside the nothing.

"Mama's here," she says, but I am lost in all that white, and have no idea where *here* is.

"WHERE COULD SHE HAVE GONE?" I ASK MY FATHER OVER dinner. I've broiled a piece of beef I bought this morning at the grocery store, a place I don't remember having been since I was small enough to ride in the cart, and I've sliced it in half between us. He microwaved two potatoes, which hissed as they cooked. Together we've shredded some lettuce into a bowl and tossed black olives into it.

It's the first real meal we've ever eaten at the dining room table without her, and it tastes good.

This afternoon, Detective Scieziesciez—whose name is pronounced, despite its hardness, despite the consonants hidden like barbs and thistles in it, simply, *shh-shh-shh*— called again, as he has every afternoon since we reported her missing, to ask if anything has turned up, changed, or suddenly occurred to us. Any more phone calls from her? Any postcards? Any lawyers serving papers?

But my father just shook his head sadly on the other

end of the line, as if the detective could see him from the downtown Toledo office he works out of.

"Nothing," my father said over and over, "nothing. Nothing."

Then, hanging up, my father said, "Thank you, Detective *Shh-shh-shh*," to the air, staring into it for a while like a man consumed with despair, a man wandering, lost, through a tunnel of despair wearing a gray prison uniform in his gray imagination.

My father shakes his head sadly now, as he did then, and grimaces at me across the table, a bloody thread of meat snagged in his front teeth. There is a familiar, watery-eyed expression on his face. He shrugs and looks down at his damaged dinner, torn to pieces on a plate.

"Your mother never loved me," he says before he picks up his fork and stabs into it again.

THEY WERE AN ATTRACTIVE SUBURBAN COUPLE. BEFORE SHE vanished, you might have seen them on a Wednesday night at Bob's Chop House. As the hostess led you to your table, you passed theirs, shushing past their silence, glancing at their salads.

Both of them had dark hair only faintly tipped with gray. Hers was shoulder length and smooth. His was whatever length and style was fashionable then for men. Not too long in back, not too tall on top. Conservative, but in touch with the times. Perhaps he was wearing the dark slacks he'd worn to work that day—half a suit: He'd have left the jacket at home.

My father's features were sharp—a sculpted nose and

deep-set eyes. My mother's cheekbones were high, and she was as slender as a girl. Flat stomach, narrow hips. Her face was always made up with a careful hand—the right tint of blush, maroon lipstick, brown eyeliner, and a beige base. The girls behind those makeup counters in the department stores she frequented knew her name, her favorite shades. Bisque, Berry, Chocolate Mousse—as if you could make a woman's face into an elegant dessert eaten off a delicate plate. Good French perfume, too, eau-de-vie—you could smell it on her if you got close.

They were well-spoken. They seemed sincere.

Still, when you saw her seated across from him at Bob's Chop House, both of them sipping rocky drinks, linen napkins on their laps, shiny silverware between them, she might look up at you as you passed by—her blue eyes flashing—and what you'd sense, if you sensed anything at all, was cold.

In truth, my mother disappeared twenty years before she did. She moved to the suburbs with a husband. She had a child. She grew a little older every day—the way a middle-aged wife and mother becomes ever more elusive to the naked eye. You look up from your magazine in the dentist's office when she walks in, but you see right through her.

And the younger woman she once was, the one you might have noticed—she became no more than a ghost, a phantom girl, wandering away in a snowstorm one day.

Or she became *me*.

Maybe *I* stepped into the skin my mother left behind, and became the girl my mother had been, the one she still wanted to be. Maybe I was wearing her youth now like an airy scarf, an accessory, all bright nerves and sticky pearls, and maybe that's why she spent so much time staring at me with that wistful look in her eyes.

I was wearing something of hers, something she

wanted back. It was written all over her face. After I turned sixteen, I couldn't bear to look at that face as it gazed into mine.

"Kat," she said one early Saturday evening in September, standing behind me at the mirror in the hallway upstairs, "you look like I looked when I was you."

I was wearing a tight black dress. Phil was taking me to homecoming. I was pinning my hair up over my neck, then letting it fall again. I had been thinking about him, how he might pull the pins out one by one in the backseat of his father's sedan and bite my neck, unzip this black dress and slip it down over my breasts. I hated talking to my mother at all, but the worst was having to talk to her when I was thinking about sex—the sexual thought suspended, half exposed in the expression and smell of it on me. It seemed, those days, that my mother was always creeping up behind me just as I was leaning into an imaginary nakedness with him, as if she'd crept up after some wet trail I'd left. When there was long, moist kissing on the television, I had to leave the room. She was always looking too hard at that kiss.

"*What?*" I asked.

"I mean," she said, "you look like I looked when I was your age," and she wandered away, seeming dazed, as if Time had just snuck up behind her and knocked her on the head with a very hard pillow.

In December, she'd turned forty-six. There were a few gray strands where she parted her dark hair, and she plucked those out with tweezers at the bathroom mirror in the middle of the night when she couldn't sleep. But she was still girlishly thin—still the same weight she'd carried down the aisle beside my father twenty years before.

There is a picture on their bedroom wall of them marrying each other. In it, my father looks sheepish and stiff.

But my mother already looks frantic, full of hate, wearing all that lightness—something white and exotic caught in an invisible net. That weight, or the absence of it, is draped in lace, and she drags a train of satin as long as winter, or the future, behind her.

And there is another photograph of her that has enjoyed a fleeting fame since she disappeared. Tacked to the bulletin board outside the supermarket, taped to the pharmacy's plate-glass window. MISSING above the picture. HAVE YOU SEEN ME?:

Suburban housewife.

Mid-forties.

A whisper of frost wound through her dark hair.

My father took that photograph himself, the one on the flyers, the one they used on the local six o'clock news. It was Christmas Day, two weeks before she vanished. She'd just opened a gift he'd given her. She peered at it under the tissue paper, as thin as pared skin, and said, "Don't worry, I'll take it back."

"Jesus Christ, Evie. What *do* you want?" he asked, the camera she'd just given him dangling around his neck.

"Surely not this," she said. And he snapped her bitter smile.

Had they *ever* had any fun? Had they *ever*, as Phil and I did, groped each other in the dark, gotten lost swimming in each other's bodies, that long kissing that turns your muscles to spilled milk, that numbness after hours of fucking, that blindness of eyes all over your body when the lights are out?

Whenever I tried to imagine it, I failed.

One early evening a few weeks before, when she and my father were out—perhaps at Bob's Chop House—I went into their bedroom and stood looking at their bed for a long time. It was, of course, inconceivable that they slept together. Or, I mean, had sex. Their *sleep* was easy enough to imagine. My father like a snoring corpse beside her, his deodorized sweat sowing salt into their sheets. My mother's tight lips parted loosely for a while, stardust gathering in the corners of her eyes before she bolted upright when the birds outside began to sing.

She was nervous, a light night sleeper who treated sleep as if it were an expensive dress that required many preparations to wear: glass of water on her nightstand, a room both warm and cool, a light on somewhere, but not on her—though, as I've said, all those afternoons right before she disappeared, there she'd be when I got home from school, folded up on her side, lost in the kind of sleep that swoops down on the sleeper in one big storm of wings and a funnel of feathers, hauling her off in its beak.

I knew what their *sleeping* beside one another for twenty years was like, but when I tried to imagine the two of them doing what Phil and I did, I saw naked statues in an art museum instead, a guard in an olive uniform standing in an archway warning you not to touch.

Their bedroom was as plain and orderly as a hotel room. A white spread, white curtains, oak chest of drawers. They had two closets, his and hers. Hers smelled like lavender soap. His smelled like leather.

I got down on my hands and knees on their gray carpet and looked under the bed. Nothing there. I opened the top drawer of the chest. Socks, a shallow dish of cuff links, a handkerchief with *BC*, my father's initials, on it.

What had I wanted to find?

Some sign of their secret life.

A condom wrapper? A dirty magazine?

I knew where my father kept those—the dirty magazines, I mean: in a file cabinet in the unfinished part of our basement beside the horizontal freezer full of yellow chicken limbs and slabs of steak gone pale with cold—a chest full of frozen hearts—and his tool bench, with his bright and expensive tools, which had the dustless look of things not used.

He kept that file cabinet locked, but I knew how to open it. Right next to the cabinet, tacked to a piece of corkboard over his tool bench, was a file card with the combination: 36-24-35.

It was like a joke—both the combination and where he kept it, precisely where anyone wanting to open the cabinet would look to find the combination for the lock— and I'd spin those ideal measurements and look at his spread-eagled Bunnies and Pets whenever I wanted.

Sometimes, my friends Mickey and Beth and I looked at them together, slipping an issue out of my father's file cabinet there in the basement, the place we retreated to whenever Mickey and Beth came over.

Down there, my parents wouldn't bother us—only, occasionally, come to the top of the stairs to shout something about dinner, or to announce that Beth's mother had called for her to come home. We could do whatever we wanted in those two rooms—the finished one, which had a gray carpet remnant covering the floor, an orange vinyl couch, a pool table no one ever used, and the unfinished one with its cement floor and white appliances humming in the emptiness. We could smoke. We could drink rum in our diet Cokes. We could look at those magazines, my father's secret Pets.

"Gross," we'd say, or, "Oh my God." But we would hold the glossy pages open for a long time, looking down at whoever she was that month—all those limbs, those wet lips. She'd look like something a wolf would eat, spread out like that, all that edible flesh, or something a hunter had shot out of the sky. When she landed at his feet, he'd jumped back in surprise with no idea what to do next.

———

But those magazines had nothing to do with my parents' secret life. That was my father's hobby, and I didn't want to think about it. Obviously, he thought no one knew what he had down there, hidden, locked up naked in the basement, waiting for him to sneak down in the middle of the night and take a peek. But in its secretness, it made him even duller, even safer, even less sexual than he already seemed.

Still, if I'd found one, found *Variations*, or *Big Boobs*, in their dresser, a place they shared, that would have been something else. That would have meant that she knew, and approved, or that they looked at them together.

Of course, there was nothing there.

I fished through the second drawer. Women's underwear. Nothing black. Nothing dirty. I looked in the third drawer, which was full of blouses she never wore. Too frilly, or too sheer, or too plain, but too expensive to throw away, and in the back, a shoe box, which I opened, and inside it a paperback book with a pink cover and raised white letters, *Achieving Orgasm: A Woman's Guide*.

I thought, *Jesus Christ*.

I pictured her scrubbing the toilet, disinfecting.

I pictured her in the kitchen, baking angry batches of cookies.

I saw her in the basement, wringing the necks of my father's white shirts while a choir of nasty children sang *"Ring around the collar! Ring around the collar!"* in her head.

I saw her in the living room running the vacuum cleaner over and over a four-inch area of carpet, seeing something in there that the huge rattling suction of her machine could not suck up, and pictured her in a bookstore in the mall on a Friday afternoon, circling a rack of books for a long time before she got up the nerve to buy that one and take it to the register.

She would have carried herself with a kind of stubborn dignity, buying that book. As the young clerk slipped it into a paper bag and handed her some change, she'd have looked him straight in the eyes and seen herself in there, wearing a camel's-hair coat, a black skirt, a silk blouse with bone buttons.

To that young clerk she must have looked like a woman with enough money to be happy (clearly, she paid another woman to manicure her nails, set her hair in smooth curls) staring at her own reflection in his eyes as he slipped this bit of bitter information about her into a paper bag—as if she'd just bought and paid for a rotten part of her own body, a limb that had been frostbitten and was putrid now, a limb the clerk was selling to her in public, in the weak light of the mall.

Pathetic, and absurd, he must have thought as he handed the book to her.

"Have a nice day," he said.

I put the lid back on the shoe box and closed the drawer.

Their marriage, I knew then, as I must have always known—their marriage was like a long drink of water so icy it turns the teeth to diamonds in your mouth.

A drink of water from a frozen fountain, twenty years long.

MY MOTHER MOVED TO THE SUBURBS WITH A HUSBAND, AND she vanished in Garden Heights. Her name was Eve, and although my father's name was Brock, not Adam, they were one of Garden Heights's first couples.

Garden Heights was an Eden without a past, like the first one—but also without temptation, or snakes, or trees. Our house was built in the middle of a cornfield in a subdivision a few miles from Toledo, and no one had ever lived in it before us, as if God had decided to re-create the world without variety this time.

Newness was the whole idea behind Garden Heights. Newness and sameness. Every house in the cornfield had been built with the same blueprint, and there was even a bylaw that prohibited the building of fences and additions. The point to the place was fitting in, and my father did.

This was a life he liked. Every night, he came home happy. "Evie!" he might say to my mother, "Guess what? I bought a raffle ticket for the board of education benefit, and won a crockpot. Look."

It was brown with a long, winding cord. For years my mother kept it above the refrigerator. Only once, she let a piece of pot roast shrivel up to shoe leather in it, and after that, she threw it out.

Or, he'd bring home the civic section of the Monday paper, and he'd show my mother his name in it: "Brock W. Connors is to be honored by the Executive Men's Charitable Foundation for work benefiting the Lion's Club of northeastern Ohio."

For weeks, he'd collected pairs of old eyeglasses, gone knock-knocking all over the neighborhood like a child's corny joke, kept them in cardboard boxes in our coat closet. When I asked him what they were for, he said they were for the poor. When I asked him what good other people's—rich people's—glasses were to the poor, he looked at me blankly, then narrowed his eyes, as if I were either very obstinate or very blurred.

In Garden Heights, my father thrived like a rubber plant left in a sunny spot and watered a lot, but my mother didn't. She was a different kind of plant entirely. A plant that could have borne thistles and juicy, dangerous fruit.

Instead, she planted petunias in our yard, and by July of every year they were dried out. Like complaints, or exasperation. Our house was stuck into some of the world's most fertile earth—black and loamy and damp—and anything could have grown there. A handful of it was as heavy as a heart, or guilt. As a child, I used to dig it up with a plastic shovel and pretend to bake cakes and cookies, shapeless pastries patted out of gravity.

That dough, that dirt, was as dark as space. For thousands of years, our backyard had been ice, and when the Ice Age ended it thawed into a swampy dinosaur forest, and when the dinosaurs got zapped by whatever zapped the dinosaurs, farmers came and turned it into farmland and country meadows, which were later bulldozed to make way for subdivisions with names like Country Meadows Estates.

Still, they'd find the skeleton of a woolly mammoth in there every once in a while as they were pouring concrete for a strip mall close by—something giant and shaggy that had gotten sucked into the ancient muck—and the sweat and blood and milk of those farmers before us could still be smelled in our backyard. The smell of yeasty manure just under the golf-course smell of lawn.

Anything could have grown there, but my mother grew petunias. I never knew what she wanted, but I knew it wasn't in Garden Heights, and it wasn't my father.

She was attractive. She walked gracefully in her high heels—but quickly, without hesitation, like a woman with a crystal dish of butter on her head. Men looked at her when we went into restaurants, staring at her ankles as we waited for the hostess, and my mother would pretend not to notice. But she noticed.

Once I saw a truck of sheep U-turn on our street. It must have been lost on a detour off the highway. I could see them from our front yard in the back of that truck— maybe fifteen sheep peeking out at me between the steel slats of that truck's trailer.

To keep from falling over as it turned too fast, those sheep had to dance. It was so pathetic, it wasn't even sad. There they were, being driven to their deaths, trying not to stumble, not to bump into each other, dancing a graceful, desperate dance of politeness.

That was how my mother looked when men looked at her.

She was getting older, but she was still attractive. When they looked at her, she noticed. And so did my father. He would glare down at his own shoes with their shiny noses.

Maybe he knew, too, that my mother wanted something.

How could he *not* know?

Those men looking at her ankles in Bob's Chop House, *they* knew.

And every afternoon and evening of those last months before she left, there she'd be, folded in half on their bed or mine, asleep like death, waking finally to the sound of canned laughter after my father got home, rising to the surface of her life like a sick aquarium fish.

When my father turned the television off, there would be nothing but the sound of flat and endless heaven above and beyond our house. Wind in a parking ramp. An empty tin can held up to an ear. It must have been unbearable. If I was off somewhere with Phil, there wouldn't even be the sound of the radio playing in my bedroom.

And then my father would climb the stairs. Loose change in his pockets—silvery, a tin bucket of forks and knives, as if a janitor were jangling his cold ring of keys toward the bedroom as winter dusk descended, earlier and earlier every night—

A man with a handful of dull bells, getting closer.

"What's for dinner, Evie?" he'd ask, and she'd roll over to look at him through her hair. His face would be lit from above. He'd switched the ceiling light on, and it blacked out his eyes and cast shadows from his sharp features down his face, as if it were cracked.

"What?" she asked, pushing her hair out of the way so he could better see her annoyed expression.

"What's for dinner? It's six o'clock." He was wearing a flannel, afterwork shirt, but he'd still have on his dress pants and his shiny black shoes, as if relaxation were something you only needed to do from the waist up.

These two decades, my father had also stayed slim. His face had aged well. He looked younger than fifty, staring down at her, but also as preserved and eternal as some frozen-faced saint painted on the wall of a chapel during the darkest Dark Age days. Pale. Uninquisitive. A painted saint gazing without judgment, or interest, at centuries of women passing by, bearing candles, or babies, or flowers in their black habits, lace veils, go-go boots, and girdles.

My father was the kind of man, like one of those expressionless saints, who sees a woman—naked, or roped in pearls, tied to a stake, or shedding tears of blood—and thinks, I wonder what's for dinner.

"Go away," my mother said. "I'll make dinner in a minute."

If he realized then that she hated him, he pretended not to notice.

Without another word, he left.

My mother could hear him in the den, changing channels on the television with the remote control again.

She rolled to her side and swung her feet off the bed, and perhaps the numbness of them surprised her on the bedroom rug. There was a mossy taste, lush and sun warmed, on her tongue—as if, in her dream, she'd eaten a butterfly.

Briefly, she might have thought of arsenic, though she didn't even know what it was, exactly, or where one bought it. But she might have imagined my father at the dinner table, hunched over his stew, turning blue, looking up at her with a pleased smile, muttering, "This is good," before he died.

It was just a thought.

Wives all over Ohio probably had them.

But the idea of murder was no more serious than the kinds of fantasies in which a suburban housewife imagines herself slapping a bad waitress, or punching a meddlesome librarian in the stomach: She is polite, she'd never do it. Instead, she might wad up a piece of gum and stick it under a chair, hoping the librarian would find it there years later and have to scrape it off with a knife.

Still, there *was* desire, there *was* poison in the air. Every night, my mother read the obituaries in silence, and I imagine she was comparing the ages of the deceased to my father's. *A lot of men die in their fifties, leaving behind a great many grieving wives.*

But my father was so robust, it must have been hard to imagine. He did not seem at all like the kind of man who might die "unexpectedly, at home" or "after a long battle with colon cancer." It might take *gallons* of arsenic to kill him, or years and years spent watching him across the dining room table, wrestling with his colon as it decayed.

One night, only a few weeks before she disappeared, my mother went down to the basement freezer to find something to feed him, her stockinged feet cold on the cement floor.

That night, the freezer light did not come on when she opened it—burnt out, she thought—but there were the usual two good steaks. A cutup chicken—twisted, yellow limbed, a little human. A pound of ground sirloin on a square of Styrofoam.

She took that out, brought it upstairs to the kitchen, and put it in the microwave for five minutes while she tossed some salad into bowls and filled a pot with water to boil pasta. She was wearing pearls, and a neat brown skirt, a soft beige turtleneck—perhaps she'd gone to the bank that afternoon to deposit my father's check—all a little rumpled from hours of sleeping in them.

The linoleum under her panty-hosed feet felt warped, blistering up along the seams, as if something humpbacked were pushing itself up from the basement. She needed to call Herschel's Furniture & Floor, and made a mental note.

When the microwave began its steady beeping, she took the pound of ground sirloin—defrosted now, heavier with its hot blood—and peeled away the plastic, tossed it into a pan, turned the gas on under it. And right away, she knew something was wrong.

Desire. Poison.

At first there was just the smell of toffee—too sweet, like a body washed up bloated on a beach. Blood and grease spat and sizzled beneath the shredded beef, but the smell grew stronger, and the kitchen filled up fast with the stench of old death, and something else—something fetid, stuffed with honeysuckle, as if a whole flock of cupids had drowned in a perfumed bath.

My mother felt dizzy with it. She had to lean against the refrigerator, and she could feel it purr against her hair.

"Jesus," my father said, hurrying in, "what stinks?" He turned the gas off under the frying pan. "This meat is rotten." He held the pan up by the black handle, then turned his face to her—curious.

"Throw it away," she said. "We have to go out to eat."

He tossed the bad hamburger, pan and all, into the garbage can under the sink, then went down to the basement and, a few minutes later called up, "Jesus, Evie, this freezer's unplugged. The whole thing's full of rotten meat."

Of course: The light had not come on.

Two days before, she remembered, she'd had to crawl on hands and knees behind the freezer to find a mother-of-pearl button that had popped off one of my sweaters when she pulled it from the dryer, and she must have accidentally knocked the plug from the socket.

"Plug it back in," she yelled.

I came home just as my father emerged from the basement.

"My God," I said, coming into the kitchen. "What reeks?"

"Shut up," my mother said, hurrying past me. "We're going out to eat."

That night, we did go out to eat. Perhaps we had Chinese. Or we each ate a steak at Bob's Chop House. Maybe we had a pizza at Mariani's. I sat between them at the table, thinking about Phil, sloshing the ice around and around in my water glass until my mother said, "Stop that."

Wherever we were, we'd eat in silence. Just a word now and then about the service, about the noisy children of the other patrons. My father might have asked me how school was going, then nodded his head while I answered in a low, bored voice.

As a family, we were vague. My mother was always in the center of her own agitation, seeming as though, far away, part of her was being chased along a dirt road by a swarm of bees. My father, on the other hand, was right there, right on the surface of the world, taking it all in too easily—the salad, the beef, the silverware—but there was nothing more to it, nothing in his world you couldn't see. And I was sixteen, trying desperately to slip into the privacy of my own mind, a place where their questions and faces could not interfere with my thoughts about sex, a place where they couldn't find me in some fantasy of naked flesh.

"What are you thinking about?" my father would ask me cheerfully as I sat there between them sawing my steak in half. "You sure seem lost in thought."

I'd imagine telling him. The sound of his utensils dropping from his hands.

But, perhaps I should have known then, I should have known that night, standing in the kitchen, that foul meat in the air—looking back on it now, I see that it was the end and the beginning of something more than dinner. More than ruined appetite, a postponed meal, a marriage strained, a freezer unplugged.

I could smell the death between them.

When my father came up from the basement, he had a look of puzzlement and blame on his face, his surprise at finding something wretched in the kitchen, cooking—something cloying and corrupted, which his wife had planned for supper.

And my mother's delicate suffering, the elegant clothes, rumpled. In a few weeks, she'd be that woman with MISSING written above her picture.

But that night, she was just the suburban wife of someone who'd wanted a simple dinner of macaroni and grease. And she'd cooked him something ghastly and mortal instead.

"What's that smell?" Phil asked when he came over to see me later that night.

"Something's dead," I said.

Phil smirked, I remember. "Is it your dad?" he asked.

AND I KNEW WHY HE ASKED IT. IN MANY WAYS, MY FATHER *was* dead. When I was only ten or eleven years old, I used to ask my father, as a joke, what the world had been like when he was alive—was there television, for instance, were there cars? Of course, I meant, when he was a *child*, and my father got the joke, and always laughed, but there was a bite to the joke, and I stopped making it after a while.

My father was, as I've said, healthy. A good-looking man. But the kind of dullness he wore like a badge—("I'm a simple man," he would say to my mother when she complained that they never went anywhere, never ate anything but steak and potatoes, and he'd say it as though it were the thing about which he was proudest, something commendable, something my mother might not have noticed if he hadn't pointed it out)—also embalmed him, ran in his veins like that gray March rain.

Every morning, he would mix a spoonful of vegetable fiber into a glass of water, stir it around and around, clunking his tablespoon against the side of the glass until that water was the color of dullness itself, and then he'd gulp it all down in one deep swallow that seemed to go on and on—

"Ah!" he'd sigh. "That's good," setting the empty glass down hard on the kitchen counter.

It was a laxative, and kept him regular, and he appreciated that.

Occasionally, after drinking this dull cocktail, he'd exhale a long, slow fart, and my mother might throw her dish towel down and mutter, "Jesus Christ, Brock."

She hated those farts.

He'd smile, big and happy, and say, "Excuse me!"

When I was ten years old, my father took me with him to his office at the Board of Education. Perhaps I'd had no school that day. Maybe I'd asked to go. Or was it his idea? Was there something there, at his office, he wanted me to see?

What I saw stunned me then. It mystifies me now:

My father was loved by women.

Old women and young women. Fat and thin. Married, single, serious women, and empty-headed flirts.

To get to his office, we had to walk down a long, gray corridor of women. I was a child. I would have been holding my father's hand. He would have been wearing shiny shoes, a black suit. Even then, he was gray at the temples, but his features were chiseled out of solid rock—not at all like a man with the kind of job he had: a job telling women what to do. Ruggedly handsome, my father spent his days at the end of a telephone with a felt-tipped pen in his hand, doodling onto a legal pad.

I'd seen those doodles.

Stars. Pyramids. Bull's-eyes. Once, a pair of women's shoes with a woman, drawn only up to her ankles, in them. Above her ankles, just air.

Still, my father had the features of a French legionnaire. An aristocrat. A mystery writer. A painter of abstractions. Give him a series of hats—a black beret, a turban, a sailor's cap—and you could have had your classically attractive anyman: sailor, artist, sultan. Instead, he was simple. Friendly. A school administrator. As he passed the secretaries who were at his disposal with their beige panty hose, soft breasts behind soft sweaters, toes pinched into skinny shoes, my father glistened.

"Good *morning*, Mr. Connors," a woman with a file folder in her hand said, fanning the folder in our direction, opening her eyes wide. "Is this your *daughter*?"

"No." My father raised his dark deadpan eyebrows at her. "Mindy, I'd like you to meet my new secretary, Kat."

Every time my father said this, and my father said this all day, a woman would open her slippery red mouth as wide as she could to laugh.

What's wrong with this picture? I thought, remembering the puzzles we puzzled out in kindergarten—

Three dogs and a toaster: *Which one doesn't fit?*

At home, my father's corniness would be met with grimaces from my mother, pain spreading itself across her face as if she'd been poked in the small of her back by a very hot pitchfork, or she'd shake her head. She might say, "Oh, please," or leave the room—or, if they were in the car together, look out the window blankly, saying nothing.

But here, his corniness was charming. Back in their break room, over cups of instant coffee and sandwiches slipped out of plastic bags and a haze of cigarette smoke winding exotic, haremlike, around them, those secretaries must have talked about my father like a pleasant, shared master. Here and there, a foot was slipped out of a shoe, tucked up under a thigh.

He could have had one or two of them, I'm sure. The skinny blond. The sweet and slightly giddy one. The one with shapely calves sashaying beneath her pleats.

Flattered to be chosen, she would have kept it quiet. She'd have met him on the sly, in a motel, black teddy stashed in her pocketbook, diaphragm already in. She'd have done whatever she could to please him in bed, just as she always tried to do his typing with a flourish, file his papers with style.

Then, back at work, she'd have kept her mouth shut. She'd have stopped lunching with her girlfriends if she had to, started keeping to herself. And when, a few months later, he broke the news that he couldn't risk it anymore—his wife was asking questions—she might have been generous enough to quit, to find a job in another office, even if it meant a bit less pay, the loss of some fringe benefit she'd grown used to having but could, finally, manage without. And, years later, when she passed him with his wife and daughter on a street in town, she would politely look down at her shoes and walk on.

But my father was far too simple for this.

His imagination was limited, and, for whatever reason, it was only my mother he loved.

I know.

I know because I was their daughter. Their only child. The product of their marriage. A soft, lopped-off part of it. I saw the looks he sent her, though he hardly spoke to her. ("A man of few words," my mother would snort at his back when he'd offered a one-word answer to some complicated question she'd asked.)

Still, for sixteen years I saw the way he passed the butter dish across the dining room table to her, as if he wished it could be more, as if he wished she could lift the lid and precious gems would spill all over her dinner, as if that might finally make her happy—an inedible, improvident gift, like easy, unexpected laughter.

There was never any of that in our house either.

"Evie, what can I do to cheer you up?" he might ask her on a Saturday when she'd spent all day complaining. He meant a movie, a drive, a quart of ice cream. She'd say, "Just pick up your dirty socks. That's all I want," and she'd be looking hard at his feet propped up on the ottoman when she said it, her jawbone making vicious little squirrel movements when she closed her mouth.

But the fact that she hated him did not seem to lessen his love for her. When she was late coming home from the mall, he'd twist the snug wedding band around and around on his finger—always conscious of her, not forgetting for a minute that he was married, looking out the window at an unfathomably high and empty sky.

He had her photo, too, enlarged, on the wall of his office, framed in oak. In it, my mother smirked into the sun at the slippery edge of a river—the Chagrin River, which ran past our subdivision, a famous river:

Once, between Cleveland and the lake, an oil glaze on that river caught fire like some stripper's slippery negligee tossed onto the water, and it went smoking through the city and its valley of warehouses, steel mills, refineries, rubber factories—through the suburbs, where the stench and the fumes and the flames were politely ignored—and it passed, then, into the country, spitting cinders into the wind, burning itself past the gawking sheep and cows, burning itself down to the great, polluted, viscous, all-forgiving mouth of Lake Erie.

That afternoon, when I was ten and went to his office with him, two or three times my father stood up from his desk, went over to that photograph on the wall, and looked carefully into it. Then he'd sit back down, seeming thoughtful, and watch the snow fall in soggy fragments of light outside.

I sat across from him. It was a long afternoon. The light from the window was so bright, we could barely open our eyes. My father tapped his pencil on his thigh, and as he did, it made a rubbery yellow blur in his hand. His desk was mahogany, buffed, with only a desk calendar, an ink blotter, a leather-bound appointment book and a coffee cup full of pens on it. I could see the elastic band of his Timex peeking out of his sleeve, cuffing his wrist with time as if he were its prisoner—time turned to x's and scattered into the void.

My father didn't seem to have any work to do that afternoon, and it bothered me. I could too easily imagine him sitting in that chair every day, watching the sky throw wet blankets all over the world—the parade of his life passing by the window with its threatening clowns, big-breasted women on the backs of white horses, asthmatic elephants wheezing in an icy rain as he tapped a too sharp pencil on his thigh.

As he tapped, that pencil made a solid, dispensable sound.

Then, after about half an hour of this, his secretary came in—all business, but her cheeks were flushed. She had on too much cheap perfume, and it trailed her in scented veils, filling my father's office with an awful sweetness, like decay. It was a smell I recognized because, during that fall, each morning on my walk to school I'd passed a squirrel that had been flattened by the tires of a car and tossed to the side of the street, near the curb, where it was slowly vanishing—

And, although, after my first glimpse of that bristled, ash-blond fur softened by blood and guts and time, I'd cross the street to avoid seeing it again, I could not avoid smelling it, and the smell of it got stronger every day—sweeter and sweeter.

More like roses steeping in sugar water than dead meat by the second week.

Like an angel's miscarried fetus by the end of the month.

Some precious rag from heaven dropped and stinking now. Lost sweetness *itself* by the side of the street.

———

This was how my father's secretary smelled, and what she reminded me of as she handed my father a pink square of paper, smiled at me, and left—thighs rubbing nylon lightly across nylon high up under her skirt as she walked. Then my father waved the little square in my direction. "You have a dentist's appointment tonight," he said. "Your mother called."

Of course, I must have known already, since she'd left the message with his secretary as my father sat in his office, only too available to talk, drumming a flaccid pencil on his pants and staring out the window, that she hadn't wanted to talk to him. But my father looked across his nearly naked desk—just those doodles on a legal pad—and said, anyway, "Guess she didn't want to talk to me."

There was that watery expression on his face.

After she disappeared, he would wear that watery mask every day.

In the morning, Phil comes over. I see him cross his yard into ours through the shallow garden where Mrs. Lefkowsky—who lived next door until she died last year—planted her hundreds and hundreds of daffodil bulbs. They're deep under the snow and frozen mud now, like Mrs. Lefkowsky herself, but I can imagine them as Phil trudges over in his big boots, that yellow writhing in the dark, a little light down there, like something you keep in the back of your mind, or buried in your backyard.

It's Saturday. My mother has been gone for one week and one day. I'd count up the hours and minutes, too, but she left on a Friday afternoon while I was at school, while my father was at work. We came home to no one. She didn't leave a note, never packed a bag, only the quick phone call the next day to tell my father she wouldn't be back, and then the nothing.

It is a serious matter, I know. The kind of thing that makes the six o'clock news, gets into the local paper. When you go to the supermarket, you see her face on the bulletin board between BABYSITTER NEEDED and I WILL SHOVEL SNOW, and you pause, look at her face, wonder briefly who she was and where she went before you stack your silver shopping cart with frozen TV dinners.

At school this week, no one said a word to me about my mother's disappearance, but my teachers seemed shy, and friendly, and even Melody Little, the most popular sophomore girl, nodded at me in the shower after gym. She looked as slick as damp plaster in the steam, but the hot water had turned her thighs fire-truck red.

It is *that* kind of serious matter—the kind that makes people who don't know you like you, speak softly to you, avoid your eyes—but for some reason, I cannot take it seriously myself. I find myself smiling, instead, all the time, laughing too hard at jokes on TV. Last night I couldn't catch my breath as Johnny Carson did a bad impersonation of George Bush, and my father looked at me sideways, his face lit up in the *Tonight Show* glow, and said, "Kat, are you really that happy she's gone?"

It wasn't an accusation. He simply wanted to know.

But after he asked me that, I thought I'd better try to start looking more serious, or troubled. Still, as hard as I try, I can't get this smile off my face.

I don't tell my father about the dreams.

Night after night I'm in a cave of snow, or my mother is calling to me but I can't find her in the whiteout all around us. I'm driving slowly over a frozen pond, hear it cracking under me, but can't open the car door to jump out. Then, there's snow in the headlights, and suddenly I'm driving ninety-five miles an hour, and she leaps into my path wearing nothing but pearls. I swerve, but I've hit something soft and solid, thrown it to the side of the road, and, when I go back to find it, it's gone.

Or the light is too bright to find it. Or a white scarf is tied around my eyes. Or the bedroom window's frozen: I can't open it. It shatters instead—luminous, flashing—and when I finally see her face, it's featureless. A helium balloon. Bloated. Her hair, you guessed it, is pure white now, like a white wig on a Styrofoam head, the kind in the window of the wig shop. She's standing on a crust of snow outside the wig shop in a white nightgown, and there's a halo hovering above her head—a band of frozen, electric stars.

They make a whirring sound, revolve into the distance as she starts to run—and that halo, like a hubcap, spins away from my tires and lands, invisible, in a snowbank in the distance.

That halo, had that really been my mother's?

When I wake up, I seem to remember my mother actually wearing a halo like it, standing above my bed in the middle of the night, and it bothers me. I wrack my memory for the details, and can't get back to sleep.

Phil wants me to see a shrink. He got the idea from his mother.

Like my father, Phil is simple.

Scratch the surface, and there's just more surface—chalk dust under your nails, but not much else. What you see, as they say, is what you get.

And this is what you see:

He has white-blond hair, which he parts in the middle, combs back over his ears. His hair is stuck in the seventies, as if he is a rerun of *Three's Company*—cute, but caught in the time warp of television. It's long in the back—at least an inch below his collar, where it curls up smoothly, ladling light. He's tall, but not broad shoul- dered, so he appears perpetually to stoop, as if he's just stepped into a room with a low ceiling, as if even the sky might not be high enough for Phil.

He thinks he is a ladies' man, and, as with the idea of me going to a shrink, I think he got this impression from his mother, who is blind. On our second date, he brought me next door to meet her, and she said, "My son is pretty, don't you think?" moving her white fingers around on his face. He pushed her away—gently, but it was a push.

Before she disappeared, my own mother said, be- mused, watching Phil cross our lawn on his way to our house, "That boy thinks he's a crumb off the loaf of love." Something in the way he was carrying himself must have made her say it. Jaunty teenage rooster. Cocky. A boy who likes the way he looks when he catches a glimpse of himself in the bathroom mirror.

Even my mother must have been, as I am, charmed by Phil—his naked pride, walking around all day with his ego exposed, the boyish vanity.

As I've said, his mother is blind, and his father left them two years ago, so Phil is now the one who leads his stone-blind mother around town by the arm.

"Here's the railing," he might say, folding her bony fingers around a railing.

"Here's the ladies' room"—placing her hand on the doorknob, looking worried as he lets her go into that dark- ness alone.

Once, their white cat, Snowman, escaped when Mrs. Hillman opened the front door to feel her way to the mail, and it ran, belly close to the ground, across the street. That cat had never been outdoors before, and it cowered stu- pidly on the front stoop of the house across the street. From the living room window, my mother and I watched

Phil go after Snowman, pick him up, and cradle him like an infant in his arms, bring him home to his blind mother.

"What a good boy," my mother said.

I'd be lying if I said I'd thought much of him, or about him, before he stopped me in the hallway of the high school one day and said he'd be moving in next door. I remember saying, "How do you know where I live?" and he'd looked hurt, as if I were accusing him of something.

"I saw you in your driveway," he said.

"Great," I said. "Welcome to the neighborhood."

He looked relieved. He looked down at my shoes, which were flat and black, a pair I left in my locker so I wouldn't have to walk around in rubber boots all day. I was wearing a maroon sweater and a pair of faded jeans, size fourteen. But my feet were small. They were the feet of a girl God had intended to be thin, but who'd mushroomed, instead, like a cloud.

Phil smiled at my shoes. "I'm looking forward to being neighbors," he said.

A few days after that first give-and-take, a week before he and his mother moved in next door, he stopped me again in the hallway. Wearing a sweatshirt that said PROPERTY OF OHIO BUCKEYES, he looked nervous, itchy, a boy with a bad burn just starting to heal somewhere you couldn't see. His hair looked yellow under the washout of the hallway's fluorescent light, and the skin above his upper lip was naked, scraped. That day, his blue eyes were naively wide and gray.

"Kat," he said, "would you want—you know—to go to that dance?"

Winter Formal.

It had never even crossed my mind that anyone would ask, and certainly not anyone with Phil's good looks and calm cool. He wasn't one of the most popular boys. He wasn't on any teams, but more than one girl was rumored to have a crush on him, to be going somewhere with him. And the popular guys seemed to have respect for Phil. He was tall, and looked strong. I would occasionally overhear those guys talking about the weekend parties that had taken place at someone's house while their parents were out of town—and Phil had been there, he'd brought beer, and had drunk it, and acted crazy. He was not obscure. The cool kids knew who he was, which, in a way, *created* him.

If every soul is just a thought in the mind of God, then every student at Theophilus Reese High School is just a thought in the minds of the cool kids. Without that, you are nothing but a gray shade, indistinguishable from the cinder block, blending into the dull shine of the lockers, something with a shadow but without substance.

Our high school was named for a farmer whose cow got loose in what was once woods and is now the football field. He chased it all day. He got thirsty, and hot, and then there was a thunderstorm, and Theophilus hid, stupidly, under a tree, which was struck by lightning. Out of the lightning, God spoke, or so the story goes, telling Theophilus to chop down all the trees and build a church.

He did, and found his cow.

Now, there are twelve hundred teenagers who go to school where that church once stood, and some of them are rich, and beautiful, and poised, and witty, and well-dressed, and always have been. When they walk down the hall together, it is like a wall of power, all ecstatic laughter and glamour.

They are like gods among the rest of us, walking faster, looking better.

And those kids knew who Phil was, but I was invisible, and fat. Why would he ask me? When he asked, I shrugged, half thinking that this was a joke, a prank his buddies had put him up to. "Sure," I said, as if I were doing him a favor—*no skin off my nose*—and he looked a bit deflated: one of those fireworks on the Fourth of July that fizzles out halfway into the sky.

That night, the night of the winter formal, I was 140 pounds of myself in a long pink dress, but Phil didn't seem to care. He walked from his house next door to get me in a rented tuxedo with big sixties lapels—brand-new but out of fashion—and he looked good in it, like a mock-up of the perfect first date. Teenage heartthrob. Lean but muscled.

My mother had taken me to buy the dress, and everything I tried on displeased her. "Your coloring is good," she often told me, by which she meant the pale skin, dark hair, blue eyes that mirrored hers, "but you're forty pounds overweight." I would step out of a dressing room with something long and ruffled on, and she'd shake her head and sigh.

Finally, the pink one was the last straw.

"Oh, well," she said, "it'll have to suffice."

And I was painfully aware of the fat as I danced: its folds, its white cream, its fluid pressure like a rain-swollen creek beneath the dress, which made noises like a thousand little girls whispering viciously against my flesh.

Garden Heights, Ohio, is not a place to be plump, to be homely, or malodorous, or scarred, or shy. There were girls from my high school at that dance in strapless black sheaths and four-inch heels. Girls as flawless as mannequins, their feet preformed to fit into their mother's expensive shoes. They didn't seem to have been born with the nuisances of blood or skin or shame.

Next to them, at this winter formal, I looked like a feminine whale, paddling the air with my thick fins, stuck between a couple of icebergs, going nowhere fast—a sym-

pathetic character, perhaps, but not lovely at all. If, to anyone, I appeared sexual, it would have been the way in
which the inside of a cat's ears are sexual. As nude as
scrubbed fruit. A glimpse of something vaguely obscene—
obscene because you hadn't wanted to see it, because you
don't want to think of something as vulnerable, as *personal*,
as a fat girl's sexuality exposed.

And Phil, in his long-limbed blue tux, seemed to be
perpetually dancing the funky chicken—arms jerking
around his shoulders as if someone were yanking at him
with strings from the sky. He thought he could dance—
believed in his abilities on the dance floor with the same
kind of stubborn confidence with which he believed he was
handsome—and, after I got over my initial embarrassment
for him, all that energy let loose like a flightless bird beneath the snuffed gym lights, I started to believe that he
could dance, too. Watching him flail in front of me as I
shuffled in front of him, I began to understand that dancing well had everything to do with believing you *could*. Like
those dreams of flying—dipping gracefully through the air
in your weightless body—if in your sleep, you stopped to
think about it for more than half a second, you'd crash like
a sack of dead ducks onto the roof of a church.

Phil didn't stop to think. He just danced.

We both danced, all night. Couldn't stop. Out of
breath within half an hour, but we danced nonstop for
three more hours.

A few years ago, about a hundred miles into the country
from our suburb, there was a farm plagued by stray voltage.
An electric current under the pasture was surging up from
Toledo Edison, shocking the cows, turning their hooves
to walkie-talkies. There was a lawsuit, and for months on
the news we heard the details over and over: The farmer's
wife lost weight, her teeth fell out, his daughter started
pulling out her eyelashes lash by lash, biting the backs of

her hands to get at the static under her skin. When that daughter closed her eyes, she said she saw sparks. And the barn cats sang terribly in the barn before they died.

But the cows danced the whole time.

Perhaps they'd been driven mad, but they danced, and there had to have been *some* joy in that. *I* had never been happier in my life than I was as I danced with Phil that night. It was as if, with Phil—dancing, or fucking, or just driving around and around in the sedan his father left him when he left—I'd finally found something to do with all the nervous tension of that suburb, which surged through the power lines between our houses and street corners like a small girl's braids pulled too tight, sending an invisible current into the air, a wave of nervous energy rising, falling, rising.

That tension—I would lie in bed some nights and imagine I heard its volts and sparks swell an invisible river above our roofs, singing a high whine in my ears, boring into my brain like a wiry nail, the whole subdivision ringing in my ears, until my head and neck would ache from the weight of so much strident silence.

Like that stray voltage, there was something raucous straining under all the politeness, all the quiet—and, finally with Phil, I found a way to move to it, or sleep through it. I bought a pair of running shoes and a green sweat suit, and when I jogged around the neighborhood—which had seemed so stiff, a stage set of a place, all edges and blades— it melted into a liquid blur, a soft backdrop of flaccid facades and sleepy trees. I let myself get thin, running in circles around Garden Heights. I no longer needed the padding. I had sex.

"ANY WORD?" HE ASKS.

"Not one." I shake my head and shut the front door behind him. Snow's coming down now in fat, gray, dirty-washcloth flakes, and they drape the lawns and trees with sluggish infant blankets. Who could blame my mother for leaving this place? The sky is falling.

And, only a few days ago, I noticed a fine layer of dust on the dining room table—the dust she had devoted her life to dusting away. It was already accumulating in gray layers, and it had only been seventy-two hours since she'd left. When I went into the living room, I saw it there, too, swirling around in the air, settling on the arms of her chairs, the coffee table, a galaxy of dust collapsing from inside itself in slow motion, burying us.

It was what she'd been doing, chasing dust, all day, every day.

So I went to the kitchen to get her feather duster with its pink plumes out from under the sink, but when I got back into the living room with it, I had no idea where to start. Dust was everywhere. It was in the light. It was in the air I was breathing. It was graying my hair. I was afraid to use the feather duster, which seemed weightless in my hands. I thought it might make it worse, kick up a whole new storm of dust that would choke or blind me. So, when my father got home from work, I said, "We have to call the Molly Maids. We can't keep this house clean by ourselves."

"I did already," he said. "They'll be here tomorrow. They'll be here every Wednesday."

"Shit," Phil says, untying the sturdy laces of his brown boots. "How could she do this to you?"

"She wanted out," I say, looking at Phil's feet.

When his boots are off, I see holes in his black socks, and each of his big toes looks vulnerable to me, raw on the beige carpet, as if two sacks of skinned mice have spilled, and Phil looks down then, too, as if he'd like to gather up those spilled mice quickly. Then he shrugs.

"So?" he asks the wall behind me, where a painting of the ocean hangs, all melancholy flotsam and churning water.

Seascape it's called. It's the only real painting that hangs in our house—a dark ocean my parents bought in a motel lobby in Toledo the year I was born, the year my father got his promotion, the one that turned his youthful energy into a heap of laundry every night at my mother's feet, the year they moved with me to Garden Heights.

STARVING ARTISTS' SALE, the sign on the highway said, and although my mother must have muttered, "That cheap junk, who wants that?" my father insisted they go, and they went. He took one look at *Seascape* and happily paid the forty dollars to own it.

Sometimes, I'd run my fingers across that canvas just to feel how thick and sticky the paint in all that choppy water was, the places the painter had gobbed on too much blue. The horizon was ominous and, with some imagination, you could smell salt, dead dolphins, weeds reeking on a beach. A thin line separated the water from the air, and though I hated the painting itself, that line was definite. Incontrovertible. There was absolute emptiness between the sea in that painting and the sky. It was a space that existed simply because nothing was in it.

"That's no excuse," Phil says.

"Who needs an excuse?" I ask.

He looks at me. There are snowflakes melting on the bridge of his nose, and his eyes are wide. I see myself in the small blue ponds of them, seeming brighter and sweeter than I am. My face is pouty and young in this reflection. I lean a little closer, looking for myself, surprised at what I see, and wonder what I'd expected: Had I expected to see my mother?

Phil looks at me strangely, looking at him, and says, "I'm worried about you, Kat. Your face looks frozen."

I try to stop smiling.

He says, "You're going to crack."

ONCE, I SAW A SHOW ABOUT EARTHQUAKES ON PBS. THERE was footage of bridges buckling and families shuffling through the open-air wreckage of what had been their homes, as a professor from Stanford explained in the background how there are huge movable plates under our continents and oceans and drugstores shifting around while we're watching television, or eating party mix, thinking about other things.

And even though the families picking through the trash for their belongings were either Turkish or from California, it seemed like a likely event to me. It seemed to me that something like it could happen to us at any time: an earthquake here in the part of the world where there were no faults, where, instead, a thick layer of mud kept our pharmacies and supermarkets and houses stuck.

Garden Heights is, as I've already mentioned, proud of its newness, the sameness of its designs, but the houses in our neighborhood seem like imitation houses. Cheaply made, pieced together overnight with materials that did not come naturally from this world—plastics, pressed woods, dry-wall.

The houses are not inexpensive, but they must have been put up hastily. Who knows what they were built on? When I stand in the kitchen, I can hear every footstep my father takes upstairs. When my mother was here, I could hear the hangers clanging in her closet while she got dressed, and every word she said to my father, and even the thin, atomized sound of her cologne as she sprayed it. When I'm quiet, I still can, as if the ceiling is made of onionskin and very flimsy hope.

Our house, like all the houses on our block, has three bed-rooms—mine, my parents', and a guest room, the door of which is always kept closed. On the rare occasions that door is opened, a cool breath of mothballs rushes into your lungs, as if the past is a guest, trapped in there for years and trying to escape.

The living room has two green-winged chairs and a floral sofa with a brocade trim, which matches the chairs, and in the den there is a tweed and over-soft couch—which is, I imagine, supposed to be the masculine parallel to the feminine living room. Informal to formal. Comfort to decorum. As though a line has to be drawn between my father's world and my mother's. Like the horizon in that *Seascape*, or the door between the finished part of the basement and the unfinished part.

The finished part has a pool table no one has ever used, the orange vinyl couch with black patches of gummy tape addressing its old wounds—something left over from my parents' poor, early married days. On weekend evenings when Phil is busy with his mother, Beth and Mickey some-times come over, and we drink Boone's Farm Apple Wine down there, look at those *Penthouses*. That wine tastes like something sour squeezed out of a May day, and after a few glasses it burns greenly behind the eyes.

The unfinished part of the basement is our family's personal wasteland: cement floor with a drain hole like a navel leading directly from our home to the sewer, the Chagrin River, then into the huge, burning cesspool of Lake Erie. Just the washer and dryer—water and air, those elements tumbling their fuzzy stars and flowers with our underwear, our socks, our soggy monogrammed towels— and a horizontal freezer full of meat and cookie dough waiting in wax paper, waiting for Christmas, waiting for my mother to bake. Fifteen cubic feet of limbo.

As we sleep, that appliance purrs beneath our beds, kicking on and off inside its strange private life like a big, dangerous pet. The great, white, humming brain of our house.

For sixteen years we have lived quietly in our suburb, with some elegance, some ease, but nothing out of the ordinary. When my mother disappeared, when I said to my father that we ought to call the police, the first thing he thought to say was, "Let's go to the station. We don't want them to come over here for all the neighbors to see. Your mother wouldn't like it."

And, of course, he was right.

My mother would have wanted to disappear without making a scene, without giving anyone anything to talk about. Every day, she worked hard to keep passion and its violence subdued in our house. From room to room, the tasteful carpet, the sturdy furniture, the neutral walls— nothing exotic, nothing bright. Even a little would have been too much, would have stood out, homely, sad, telling the story of her discontent, letting guests know she'd wanted—once imagined—more.

A Chinese vase, a rug of embroidered roses, even a peacock feather would have revealed my mother—naked,

longing—for the whole world to pity. She knew this because she'd been to houses like that, the houses of women
who served European teas, though they'd never been to
Europe, and if they ever did go to Europe, they would see
it through the tinted windows of an air-conditioned bus,
watching the castles and the Alps roll by, too blurred in
the distance to appraise.

There's only so much beauty women like that can
bear. You see them at the Grand Canyon, the Pacific
Ocean, Niagara Falls, holding the hands of their bored
children—who, having been presented with some wonder
of the world are drop-jawed with awe at something alto-
gether wrong: the hot dog that fell on the ground, roiling
with red ants, or the retarded man with unzipped pants, or
the metal railing that surrounds it, fences the awe itself,
keeps the tourists from falling in. They want to make a
balance beam of that, to walk the space between death and
their safe American vacation, and who could blame them?

The children are just bored, but it is their mothers
who can't bear to look at the thing itself.

Not out of fear. No. They're too far removed for fear.
There are signs to tell you when you're too close to the
edge, bronzed lifeguards blowing whistles when you've
swum too far. There are rangers in uniforms—and, below
you, the *Maid of the Mist*, drifting into the cool kiss of it,
then veering back just in time.

Fear would make sense. But it's something else. A ta-
boo. An inhibition. A kind of modesty imposed on the
natural world by women. Their husbands might be gawking and snapping photos, but the wives call them back to
the station wagons and their sandwiches and soft drinks
stashed in picnic baskets.

And the suburbs are full of homes like those, decorated by women like that. It gave my mother a seasick chill
to look to the bottoms of their wistful teacups, to smell
the rueful, steeping leaves sinking to the bottoms of their

hand-painted kettles. The pursuit of exotic beauty in such a life would have been like having a ball of tinfoil in your stomach, all that airy metal filling you up with hunger.

And my father was not an exotic man. He'd never been to war. He'd never sailed the sea. He'd grown up in a suburb like the one we lived in now. A life without crisis, or wild-life.

Oddly, he owned a rifle, which his father had inherited from his own father, and which he kept in the basement but never used. He seemed, in fact, afraid of his own rifle. It was kept unloaded, locked up in the same cabinet where he kept his collection of dirty magazines. Like my father's masculinity, it was useless, and unusable, in the basement beneath our feet. Just something he'd inherited from some earlier era, the manlier man of his father's father, who must have been a hunter, who must have known how to skin a buck.

Once, my mother went downstairs to put a load of laundry in the washer, and surprised him. He was holding that rifle in his arms like a child.

When she saw him, she said, "Put that thing away," and he did.

My father was a man who spent his days in an office, doo-dling, wearing shiny shoes, tapping a pencil on his thigh. All that testosterone surging and spiking like bees in the blood, and not a thing to do with it. On Saturdays, he chased little balls over a long slope of lawn with brilliant clubs, came home red-faced, frustrated, badly beaten, hardly a man at all.

"Beige," I remember my mother saying to the painters who stood in our living room one summer afternoon years ago—two fat men in overalls holding brushes. It was June, and the windows were open. Outside, a sprinkler whirred in rusty spinning, and a domesticated dog yelped wildly for a moment, then stopped. Somewhere someone was practicing a flute, playing scales over and over, perfect and shrill, like a kind of obedient screaming.

"You could try something else, ma'am. Something different. Shell pink. Or a light blue," one of them offered.

But she just shook her head.

PHIL HAS THE NAME OF A SHRINK WRITTEN DOWN ON A PIECE of yellow paper—

Dr. Maya Phaler: 878-1675.

He hands the piece of paper to me.

"My mom's been seeing her ever since my father split. She says it helps a lot." Phil says this as he walks toward the stairs to my bedroom. He says, "You need to get your anger out."

I follow him, holding my square of yellow.

Phil lies back on my bed, propped up by the pansy-covered pillows, and he looks, worried, at my ceiling. I sit by his feet and rest my hand casually on his ankle. There, the bone feels hard—a sharp rock slipped into his sock—but he moves it away from my hand as if I've pinched or tickled him. Then he rolls over and opens the top drawer of my nightstand, where I keep the cigarettes and condoms and contraceptive foam.

That foam is like something a virgin might find in her mouth one summer morning at the seashore. It's immaculate, and smells like nothing.

But he's going for the cigarettes, I know—a fresh, soft pack of Marlboro Lights—and he spins the thin cellophane ribbon around the top in one clean movement, like slitting a fish, but he hands it over to me when he can't get a cigarette out, jammed together as they are, dry and white.

I scratch one out with my nails and pass it to him. When his fingers touch mine, I snag them and pull his hand to my lips. He has to sit up a little for me to kiss the tips.

I look into his eyes, and say, "Want to have sex?"

But Phil glances back at the ceiling quickly and falls again into the pillow, shaking his head. "No," he says. "I want to talk about this shrink."

It's an excuse, I think, not to have sex, but I let him talk.

When it comes to talk, Phil isn't much. He'll pause, look soulful, pound a fist on his knee when he really means something, and you can see he means something, but what it is, well, that's often lost in a fog of generalizations and half-finished sentences. Listening to Phil talk is a bit like watching golf on television. You see he's got the moves, nice clubs, appropriate outerwear. You can tell when the sun's in his eyes. You can see the pressure's finally getting to him. But no matter how carefully you watch, you'll never see him hit the ball, and you'll never see it land.

This has never bothered me. Like my father, Phil is simple, and his inarticulateness goes with this like a sprig of parsley on a Salisbury steak. His monologues are full of vivid and amusing misstatements, the mangling of clichés. Once, complaining that his mother tried to do things that blind people should not attempt, like lighting candles at Christmas, he said, "My mother wants to have her blindness and eat it, too."

I imagined Phil's mother spooning blindness into her own open mouth like devil's food cake. But without texture or weight. Bittersweet and rich.

Another time he said, regarding his father's late support checks, that calling him in Texas wouldn't help, it

would just make the checks even later. "It's a vicious circus," Phil said.

When I asked if he thought that perhaps writing a
letter, explaining their situation—the mortgage payment
late again, the electric company calling—might help, he
said, "I'm virtuously certain it wouldn't," looking martyred
and older than his years.

First Phil bites his lip. Then he smokes. Then he says,
"This is too much for you to deal with, you know, alone.
This is, your mom taking off. It's a heavy thing, you know.
You need someone to talk to about this load."

I wait. When he doesn't say anything else, I say, "Is
that all?"

"Yeah," he says. There is a rope of smoke around his
fist. He looks at it.

"Fine," I say. "I'll call the shrink. Want to have sex?"
I don't want to talk to Phil about my load. I want his skin
to expand and contract like a human sack over mine.

He shakes his head no.

He moves his foot away from my hand completely,
and I look down at my own feet, bare on the white carpet,
peeking out of footless black tights.

Since I hit 122 pounds last month, I've started wearing
Flashdance clothes. Little, loose skirts. Canvas shoes and
bodysuits. A few weeks ago my father looked at me in one
of these new outfits. He'd come downstairs while I was
making toast for breakfast, the kitchen smelling like smoke
and Wonderbread, and my father said, "Kat, you're not
doing anything, you know, to make yourself thin?"

"I jog," I said. I shrugged, smiled.

But he looked worried, his face as long as a horse's
looking at my ankles, and I realized he must have seen a
show about bulimia or anorexia. He must have thought I
was gagging up breakfast after he dropped me off at school.

Maybe he was worried that I would get thinner and thinner, until I became as unfindable as my mother, and I felt a stab of compassion for him, imagining my father alone in this house with the white shadows of his two invisible women. I remembered how, one summer, he'd taken a whole roll of photographs of my mother and me. "I want to show off my pretty girls at work," he'd said, and my mother had agreed to pose with me in the backyard.

He had us stand with the sun in our eyes, squinting into his camera, and kept motioning us backward, to get us in the frame, until my mother finally got mad and said, "I'm not moving again."

He took picture after picture.

But the film came back from the camera store blank.

"I'm sorry," the clerk in the camera store said, "your photos didn't turn out, Mr. Connors." My father didn't understand why. He insisted on seeing the blanks for himself, though it took the clerk a long time to find them in the wastebasket where they threw the bad prints away.

"Here," he said finally. "You don't have to pay for these, of course."

"Of course," my father said, but he stood looking at his envelope of blanks—bright, empty squares without us in them.

"All that trouble for nothing," my mother said.

"Dad," I said, and squeezed his upper arm, which felt surprisingly muscled under his blue blazer, "I just used to eat too much."

He nodded. He said, "That's what your mother always said."

DR. MAYA PHALER LOOKS LIKE AN ACTRESS PLAYING THE part of a savvy, worldwise shrink, like someone pretending to be an expert on something she doesn't know one thing about. I think of *Marcus Welby, M.D.*—an interview I saw once in *TV Guide* with the white-haired, grandfatherly guy who played that part, how he'd told the interviewer that people would routinely come up to him on the street and, instead of asking for an autograph, would ask for medical advice.

Dr. Maya Phaler even has a pair of silver spectacles dangling from a silver chain around her neck. Not like an old lady or a librarian, though. Like an actress, as I've said—as though the costume people decided she needed a finishing touch. A psychologist's prop.

Blonde. Maybe fifty years old—but California blonde, like Phil. If it isn't natural, if it's a dye job, she's gone to great trouble and expense to get it right.

Hers is a class act all the way. Even her shoes are dead-on. Psychologist shoes: black, low-heeled, but with tasteful little bows, also black, just above her toes. She's wearing a two-piece suit the color of key lime pie, and the skirt is well above the knee, revealing slender legs, curvaceous calves—though, just above her right ankle, beneath the beige panty hose, I see a Band-Aid: A bit of recklessness perhaps? A woman in a hurry? This morning she must have slipped in the shower with a razor in her hand.

"Katrina?"

I say, "Kat."

She's looking at my insurance card: Although she charges a hundred dollars an hour, I'll never see a bill.

"Anxiety disorder" it says on my paperwork—(Is that what it is when you can't stop smiling? Didn't they used to call that joy?)—and it's covered by the benefits my father gets from the board of education. Full mental health coverage—an attempt, I imagine, to keep underworked and overpaid administrators like my father from going nuts and busting up the place.

Though, as far as I know, my father has never seen a shrink.

Nor has my mother—

Though, clearly, my mother could be anywhere right now, doing anything. She could be visiting a shrink, or at a shrink convention, or studying to be a shrink herself, for all I know. At Harvard. Or Berkeley.

This is the way I've begun to think. Every morning I lie in bed and imagine the most absurd place my mother could be.

This morning, the Shrine circus came to mind, which led me to imagine my mother in sequins, brandishing a whip in a cage of yawning tigers. I pictured her going back to a trailer with a clown after the show was over, helping him take off his makeup with a blob of cold cream on a rectangle of Kleenex.

But when the makeup was off—that greasy frown—I couldn't envision a face for my mother's new lover. It was as if she'd wiped his face off with the makeup, and he was looking in the mirror for it as my mother filed her finger-nails behind him. A clownish blank.

"Katrina's a nice name," Dr. Phaler says, fingering the chain that holds her spectacles. "You don't use it?"

"No." I shake my head too slowly—perhaps I appear despondent. With a lighter tone I add, "My mother wanted to call me Kat. She wanted a cat."

Dr. Phaler doesn't laugh.

"So, on the phone you said your boyfriend suggested you see me. How can I help?"

The question throws me. I hadn't thought of myself as here for *help*. I'd imagined I was here to *defy* analysis, to banter wittily with a professional about my personal life until she managed to wrestle some kernel of truth out of my clenched fist, weasel some secret out of my subconscious mind. Remember *Spellbound*?

Surely I, too, had something extraordinary repressed, something Dr. Phaler was being paid a hundred dollars an hour to find—the way Ingrid Bergman forced Gregory Peck to remember how he'd slid down a banister into his brother's back as a child and impaled him on a gate.

Gregory Peck held his head a lot during his long psychiatric sessions, trying to keep it in, twisting around in close-up after close-up, looking exquisitely tortured—all that guilt and grief—while Ingrid Bergman kept on needling him. Couldn't Dr. Phaler do something similar for me, shine her professional flashlight to the bottom of that well, that quiet ice at the center of myself, where *my* guilt, or grief, or anger, or mother still was?

Then, I'd have a good long life full of healthy relationships and mature responses to life's inevitable ups and downs—spared all the psychosis and neurosis for which I am otherwise headed:

The frigidity, or nymphomania.

The handwashing.

The hair twirling.

The drive to fail, or the compulsive need to achieve.

Perhaps I could dredge my memory, the way Peck did, and make some room in there so I could *heal*, or *begin the healing process.*

Except that there doesn't seem to be much dark mystery in there to dredge.

I've tried.

Over and over.

Night after night.

There must be *some* reason I feel nothing.

Surely it is not just that *I feel nothing*.

Surely I am suffering some exquisite torture, too. I am sensitive. I am good. Surely I am a victim of something, not nothing. I am not merely devoid of feeling, am I? I must be *troubled*. The troubled are everywhere. There are books and television shows and whole industries devoted to them—magazines for them to read, hot lines for them to call, uplifting magnets to stick on their refrigerators. They surround us, loving too much, crying real tears, confessing their sins and being forgiven.

But there are no twelve-step programs for people who are selfish, or heartless, or shallow, as most people seem to be. There are no Monday night movies about girls who aren't troubled at all.

Instead, the girls on the Monday night movies are fragile, and big-eyed, and too sensitive for this world, and the bad things that happen to them bother them a lot. Their beauty is the beauty of suffering endured. You can always see their collarbones under the flimsy dresses they wear, and darkness gathers there.

But I have never been able to imagine myself in one of those movies. Until my mother left, my life seemed ordinary, and dull, and untroubled. No "funny" games with uncles. No vague memories of my father torturing my childhood pets. I never had any childhood pets. Just a glimpse here or there of my mother in a bathrobe, looking annoyed. A few dull family outings—my father with a fishing pole, my mother running after a paper napkin that got loose from the picnic basket and flew across the park. There was a trip out West when I was five. I had to get out of the car to pee in the desert and got red dust on my knees. When I climbed back into the car, I asked my father where we were.

"Death Valley," he said.

I slept all the way to the ocean while a groggy wand of sun moved back and forth across my face.

I remember a beesting at Great Serpent Mound National Park one summer. A twisted ankle at the circus. A Jujube caught in my molar at the movies: I had to go to the rest room to dig it out.

Nothing. Less than nothing. A childhood without trauma. Who ever heard of such a thing?

Even now, I feel just lightness when I consider my life, even more lightness than ever now that my mother's gone, as if I am carrying a hollow cake with me wherever I go, balancing it on a tray that wants to sail out of my hands like a kite in wind.

What can an analyst possibly analyze out of such a life?

But that's exactly how it is in the movies: You resist all the lust and tenderness and terror, while your shrink ice-picks at you until your head's been cracked.

"I don't know," I say. "I guess you helped Mrs. Hillman when her husband left—"

Nothing from Dr. Phaler. Not even a nod. Patient/doctor confidentiality, I suppose. She can't even clear her throat.

"And, I guess, well, my mother left."

Now she cocks her head as if she's heard a flute note in the distance.

A few seconds pass.

She says, "Your mother left."

I lift and drop my shoulder. The left one. The side of reason, and control.

Or is that the right?

I'm looking at her knees, which are like the flat faces of two owls.

"Yeah," I say. "Yes."

"Where did she go?" Dr. Phaler asks.

"That's an excellent question," I answer.

TWO

JANUARY 1987

"I'M UP HERE!" I HEAR HER SHOUT.

"Over here!"

"Down here!"

It doesn't matter. I'm locked in. I pound my fists on the lid of this—whatever it is—until my hands ache. She's out there, telling me finally where she is, but I'm stuck in this cold, locked box. This void. This square cut out of winter air with a pair of very sharp shears.

When I wake up, there's snow spitting under my window shade, melting mid-bedroom, and I remember opening my window before I went to bed, desperate for fresh air because the smell of her perfume—eau-de-vie—wafting down the hall, leaking up under my bedroom door, had been so strong I thought that I might choke to death on the scent of my mother in my sleep.

IT'S A YEAR TO THE DAY SINCE SHE LEFT—WITHOUT A WORD, without a trace, without her coat, without her purse, without so much as a glass slipper dropped behind her in the driveway, run over, crunched to glittering Cinderella bits.

The first few months she was gone, Detective Scieziesciez would call every few days to ask, again, if we had heard from her, and to assure us that *he* hadn't. The flyers his people put up all over town—the ones with her photograph, poorly reproduced, grimacing into my father's camera on Christmas morning—were taken down or blew away in the winter wind. No one even called with some crank clue, some paranoid theory linking my mother's disappearance to the sighting of a UFO over Lake Erie.

What can you do? It's a free country. If a grown woman wants to disappear in it, she can. None of the authorities we've spoken to has had any authority over this kind of thing, the kind of thing involving women who turn to dust in the suburbs and sweep themselves up. God knows, as the saying goes, where she's gone. And He's not talking.

Nor have any of the authorities expressed much concern. When we went to the Bureau of Missing Persons, everyone we spoke to took out a blank sheet of paper and wrote my mother's name at the top, then wrote "Adult White Female" underneath it, as though that might conjure her up.

If anything, I imagine they felt sympathy for her. Looking up from that blank sheet to my father's face, down at that emptiness again, they might have been able to imagine her life, and hoped she'd managed to escape.

"We see a hundred cases of missing wives a week," a missing persons secretary said, laying a hand on my father's hand, as if it would make him feel better. She had fingernails as long as hooks, a paperback book hidden under her telephone switchboard, *Women Who Love Too Much*, and she snuck it back out before we'd even left her desk. It seemed, that year, that every secretary in every office had that book on her desk, spine broken.

When she smiled good-bye her teeth looked false and bright.

Just once, Detective Scieziesciez came to the house. It was morning, and my father had already left for work. "Dad," I'd shouted down to him from the upstairs bathroom while he was huffing around in the hallway waiting for me, "just go. I'll walk. I'm going to have to be late."

"Are you sure, Kat?"

He said it generously, but I could tell he was annoyed. His voice sounded thin, transparent, like a piece of cloth stretched tightly over the mouth of a jar.

Tardiness, in my father's book, was a sin right up there next to homicide, although I knew he wouldn't reprimand me for it. Always, we'd had a polite relationship, but since my mother disappeared, it had become even more so. It had become something formal, Victorian, lacking even the intimacy of irritation. When I said I didn't feel well, didn't want to go to school, or was going to be late, he never asked me why, and I suspected it might be because he was afraid I might tell him I'd gotten my period, and had cramps, or some other terrible embarassment from which neither of us would ever fully recover.

That morning, I was running late for school because I'd spent too much time trying to decide what to wear. I was upstairs, standing in the bathroom with a pile of my own discarded clothes at my feet, naked except for a flowered bra and matching panties. It had been months since my mother left, and the last thing I expected was that Detective Scieziesciez would pull up unannounced in his unmarked car.

I heard a knock on the door, and I peeked out from under the mini-blinds in the bathroom window, and I could see him pacing around down there on our front steps in a trench coat, smoking a cigarette, looking up toward the bathroom window.

I dropped the blinds, grabbed a red turtleneck sweater and pulled it on, a plaid skirt and pulled it up—a kind of schoolgirl costume I'd never truly considered wearing to school—and I ran barefoot down the stairs.

Detective Scieziesciez knocked, again, hard and insistently on the front door as I was opening it, and he lost his balance briefly, knocking on the emptiness, stumbling into the house, and looking like a handsome actor playing the part of a detective—dark-haired, maybe forty years old, five o'clock shadow dusking his strong jaw, though it was still only early morning.

I was impressed by that shadow, that implication of unbridled beard. It made Detective Scieziesciez look like a man with such a surplus of virility he couldn't possibly shave it off. I'd never actually seen him in the flesh, just listened to his husky voice on our answering machine, seen his letters lying on the kitchen table where my father left them—official messages regarding the ongoing investigation into Eve Connors's disappearance, which was being handled with appropriate gravity and attention (although, in those letters, often her name was misspelled as Eve *Conyers*, or *Eva* Connors).

He introduced himself, asked if he could have a look around.

As I've said, I was impressed by the five o'clock shadow, the trench coat, the smell of fresh smoke on the detective, but I was also a little annoyed. It was almost spring. My mother had been gone since January, and it seemed crazy and unreasonable to want to search the house at such a late date. If there'd been a murder weapon on the kitchen counter—a big, bloody spoon—we'd had plenty of time to find it ourselves.

Still, the detective looked damp and sexy wiping his muddy shoes on our rug. I looked down at those muddy prints, affected. Although I realized that I shouldn't just let this stranger in without checking some kind of ID—a badge, passport, dog tags?—I stepped out of his way and let him pass me in the hallway. The idea of not letting him in seemed more foolish than letting him—as if, while standing on the deck of the *Titanic*, I'd been offered a seat on a lifeboat and decided not to take it because I was afraid it might spring a leak.

I could smell deodorant soap under his coat, and inhaled as much of it as I could as he passed.

It had been a long time since I'd felt excited—sexually or otherwise. Some time in February, it seemed, a kind of spongy numbness had settled into my imagination, a physical numbness in my brain, not unlike the rather pleasant exhaustion one feels after a long, hard hike. I slept hard every night, never daydreamed, rarely worried about anything more than what to wear to school. I thought, perhaps, that I was becoming more like my father. Food tasted good. Television entertained. Work was work. Time passed, and the weather changed.

And sex seemed unnecessary. Phil and I were still together, still a recognized high school couple, still spending our lunch period together, whispering through study hall, smoking cigarettes in his father's car on the short drive home from school, but we hadn't had sex since my mother disappeared, never took our clothes off in one another's presence again, almost never even kissed.

At first, it had been Phil who seemed to have changed.

That whole first year, he'd wanted to do nothing except fuck. I'd have just climbed into the passenger seat of his father's sedan, and already he'd have his hands inside my shirt, moving around fast, as if he'd lost something slippery in there. When we parked in the empty lot of some strip mall late at night, the windows would steam up like the snake house at the zoo—the deep weedy humidity of reptiles crawling over and under one another behind glass aquarium cases, and the night around that sedan would be a darkening green, closing down on us like eggs in a huge, watering mouth.

Then, suddenly, Phil wanted nothing—no physical contact at all.

For Valentine's Day I bought a red satin bra and panties at the mall and invited him over. But he looked sad when he saw them.

"I don't feel very well," he said, and I put my clothes back on.

When I looked out my bedroom window I could see something small and blond-furred down there that had been run over in the road. It made a red sash of blood in the snow between two tire tracks. The naked trees were fringed with a loose, bluish fog. It looked like a Valentine—beautiful, brutal, cold—and my sexy underwear seemed to burn against my skin.

I was horny—a word I'd always hated, with its connotation of clumsy eagerness and need—and felt humiliated, standing there at the window, by my desire. It had only been a few weeks since my mother had vanished, and those first few weeks I wanted sex more than ever. I thought about it constantly—in bed, in the shower, in Great Books, in the passenger seat of my father's car as he drove me to school.

And then one day my desire was simply turned off like a faucet, as if someone had called the water company while I was gone, and when I got back home, there was nothing but a dry, sucking sound when I tried to turn it on.

But as I watched Detective Scieziesciez's back as he passed through our living room I could imagine straddling his hips in my mother's armchair, my hands in his hair, my mouth against his. It was as if Detective Scieziesciez shed a subliminal mist of maleness into the air as he passed—musky, intoxicating.

Perhaps, I thought, he had a gun under that trench coat, and knew how to use it. Perhaps, I thought, something exotic might happen right here in our Garden Heights home with Detective Scieziesciez in it.

Detective Scieziesciez looked around the kitchen, turned, smiled at me, and said, "Have your dad call me when he gets back, sweetheart."

"Is everything okay?" I asked.

"Everything looks perfectly normal here," he said, gesturing toward the kitchen, where the Formica glowed in the sterile morning light. "Perfectly in order—but, of course, in a case like this, we have to double-check every little thing."

"Double check," I repeated in my head, "every little thing." It was absurd, of course, since my mother had been gone since January, and this was the first we'd seen of the detective, the first visit we'd had from any authority what-soever. *Double*-checking didn't seem to be what he was up to, let alone *every little thing*, since he'd spent hardly five minutes in the house.

Still, I was hoping he'd come back. When I opened the door to let him out, the early spring air smelled bla-tantly of sex: snails and garlic and muck.

MY FATHER CALLED THE DETECTIVE THAT EVENING WHEN HE got home from work, and when I asked what he'd wanted, my father said, "Detective *Shh-shh-shh* wants me to take a lie detector test."

"*You?*" I asked. The word shot out of me like a bat flying fast and blind into a picture window. I looked at my father's pale plate of a face—the face of a man who took an absurd amount of pride in never having told a lie, his face like a bare lightbulb, all nakedness and surprise. My father couldn't hide anything in the plainness of that.

Once, my mother accused him of lying to her about

the price of a strand of pearls he'd bought for her birth-day—she didn't believe they were as expensive as he said—and she'd held them up to the light of the kitchen window, looking hard.

"How much did they cost, Brock?"

"Seven hundred dollars," he said, sounding defensive, maybe even a little desperate, as if he were being inter-rogated by the police about a crime he had committed years before, a crime he thought we'd all forgotten about by now.

"You couldn't have spent more than four hundred dollars on these," she said, fingering each one critically. "You're lying." And she made this last statement with a kind of exuberant satisfaction, turning to fix him with her eyes.

"I've *never* told a lie," my father said, and he looked angry, backing out of the kitchen. I pictured him then with George Washington's white wig on his head, an ax in his hand and that expression on his face.

My father's face was *so* unlike the face of Detective Scie-ziesciez, who looked sneaky in a calm, professional way, as if his sneakiness were sanctioned by the state. Detective Scieziesciez looked like a man who could pull the wool over your eyes for a long time—winking, calling you sweetheart, looking soulfully into your hungry eyes. He was a man of an entirely different order than my father—or, I thought, Phil.

A *man*.

Suddenly, I'd become aware of the line between men and *men*. Men with badges and hammers, and men who doodled all day on legal pads. Men who'd been to war, and men who'd studied accounting. And it was the former I found myself interested in. I found myself staring hard at jocks and cowboys on television—men with balls and hel-mets, or horses and whips, men who ate their dinners with their fists, always in a hurry, not two words for their women or their fans. After so many years of hearing and believing that men should be gentle, and sensitive, good listeners, wearers of slippers.

Late one night I watched a television show about some archaeologists who found a Mammoth Man frozen in a block of ice. The archaeologists were afraid the ice would melt, and Mammoth Man would step out of it alive. On television, they were panicked, but in our living room in Garden Heights, I felt giddy with possibilities. Under that ice, you could see he was wearing only a loincloth, and he was carrying a club. I could imagine the smell of him as he melted—hairy seaweed, filth and microbes, the wet dog smell of snow turning into mud.

"Teach Your Man How to Talk About His Feelings" the women's magazines at the grocery store screamed at the check-out line, but why? I was tired of feelings being talked about. All this talk about feelings, it made children out of adults, adults out of children. Instead of men with their emotions, I started thinking about men with guns. Men in trenches. Hunters, and cops, and Vietnam vets. Men who kept their dangerous feelings to themselves.

I thought maybe Detective Scieziesciez was a Vietnam vet. Maybe he had flashbacks. Maybe he closed his eyes at night and saw whole villages burned up, his buddies blown to damp balloon bits by land mines. Maybe he carried all that with him when he walked down the street in Toledo. Unlike my father, unlike Phil, Detective Scieziesciez might not be safe. He might have committed atrocities in the name of democracy, killed children, raped women, just to protect places like Garden Heights, Ohio, so dull suburban people like us could have VCRs and TV dinners.

I thought of the first policeman I'd ever seen up close—Officer McCarthy—who'd come to our fifth-grade class to lecture us against taking drugs we'd never considered taking, never even heard of. I remembered the way that cop had stood, shrugging and armed, before us, cautioning us not to sniff things we had no idea we'd want, so desperately, to sniff—trying to imagine ourselves, in that classroom, as he chatted on and on about *high* and *stoned* and *dead* as a series of white kites above Ohio cut loose from the twine.

Seeing Officer McCarthy in his uniform had stirred something inside me as Detective Scieziesciez had stirred me that morning. Officer McCarthy, I thought, was the kind of father I wanted—the kind who wore a uniform and dodged bullets all day. The kind who could fix the broken chain on your bike, who'd take his uniform off after work to do it, roll up his sleeves, get grease on his face, swear, and make a mess instead of reading a newspaper in an armchair for hours, sipping Bacardi out of a flashing glass, stiff with the kind of stress no child could comprehend— the kind of stress that loosens a man's muscles instead of strengthening them.

I wanted the kind of father who might guard the house at night with a gun, who could predict which way a storm would head, who would stand up to my mother when she insulted him to his face, who was able to tell a lie.

Men killed things, and women cooked them. It had been that way since Mammoth Man. It was the way things were meant to be.

But neither Phil nor my father had ever killed a thing. Maybe one or both had run over a possum on the highway, but they'd have felt pretty bad about it, a little sick. They didn't hunt, or fish, or trap. I doubted my father, in fact, had ever once touched raw flesh with his hands. It was always my mother who'd cooked the meat. Those violent pounds of ground round. Cut-up chickens. That dark, cold place inside a turkey, the one you have to reach up into to pull out the plastic bag of livers and gizzards—frozen, awesome.

My father could never have put his hand up there. If we'd had to count on my father to hunt down dinner, or butcher it, or stuff it, we'd have starved to death long ago.

He didn't even barbecue.

As far as I know, in all the years they were married, my father never made himself a meal. And after she left, he might tear up some lettuce, open a can of olives, but he needed me to go to the grocery store, buy our bloody dinners, and bring them home.

"Why would they ask *you* to take a lie detector test?" I asked my father, incredulous.

"It's standard," my father said, "in cases like this, I guess." And he shrugged, looking lost.

The test was never mentioned again. My father never told me when he was going to take it, or what they'd asked him when he did, but a few weeks later a woman called from the detective's office and left a message on the answering machine, very cheerfully, like a doctor calling to let you know whether you're pregnant or not.

"Mr. Connors, you passed your lie detector test. Detective *Shh-shh-shh* wanted to let you know that any further investigation of this sort has been called off."

I listened to the message when I got home from school, feeling relieved at the tone of the woman's voice, the happy results of my father's test—maybe even a little proud, uplifted, as if my child had been elected treasurer or secretary of the student council, a position without glamour but carrying with it a few modest responsibilities—and I left it on the machine so my father could hear it for himself. When he came home, I said, "There's a message for you," pointing at the blinking red light by the phone, and I stood behind him as he played it, then erased it, and then he looked at me without expression.

"Whoopdeedoo," he said.

WHEN SPRING FINALLY ARRIVED IN FULL, WITH ITS MUD AND swampy grass and the pregnant dancing of robins in puddles, I couldn't help but think my mother might show up again. The snow would melt, and there my mother would be in the backyard, where she'd been all along. Blossoms on her branches. A nervous bird's nest pecked and braided in her hair—

Not that I think she's dead, not that I believe for a moment that she could be resurrected, but I do believe, wherever she is, *whatever* she is, my mother has changed.

Of course she has.

It's been a long time, and everyone changes. Especially women. I imagine her returning as a younger woman. Paper-skinned, exquisite, carrying a pail of white cherries with her, each one with a worm curled sleepily around its pit.

Or I imagine her coming back as an old woman, rocking in a rocking chair, knitting socks all day—surrounded by piles of those moist, breathy socks.

Even in my dreams, she bears only the slimmest resemblance to the mother I thought she was.

That January, a year ago, when my father first told the police about the argument they'd had, about the phone call from her the next morning, how she'd vowed never to return—when he went on and on in that trembling voice, told the three cops who sat in a blue row in front of us how her own mother had done the same thing, run off on a husband and daughter in the middle of an ordinary afternoon, and how, for months, she'd been acting strange, how she'd bought a miniskirt and a canary and started slipping away for hours without explanation, or sleeping in the middle of the day like a woman who'd been dredged out of a bog, they'd asked if he thought she might be dead. They'd asked if he thought she could have been suicidal, could have done something permanent and rash.

The mouths of those policemen looked as though they'd been wired too tightly. Even when they smiled reassuringly at us, their lips stayed linear, corners pulled back, making a flat line in the middle of their faces.

My father looked at me. I was sitting next to him on a folding chair in one of these officers' offices. Both of us had our hands folded in our laps as if we were praying or holding on to butterflies—cupped loosely, secretly between our palms—and I just shook my head.

No, I thought then, and still think now. She isn't dead. The world's too full, still, of my mother. I think of a pile of leaves my father left raked last fall in the backyard, but forgot to bag, to have hauled away—

Those leaves sank back into the earth after only a few months of rain and snow. They turned first into a layer of thatch, melting into each other, becoming one thing—a thin black mattress that seemed to exhale a cool but festering breath. Then, they started to shrink, curl up, absorbing light like skin, as if you could dig there and find night itself in the center. And then one day they were simply gone, merged with the earth, swallowed up, a damp shadow, something as thick as gravy spilled where they'd been.

Looking into that, I felt my skin crawl with maggots, with the kind of soft, toothless insects that get into your body when you have no more use for it, and shivered.

It's impossible to imagine my mother like that. I cannot imagine her softened, thawed, decayed, becoming sweeter as she spoils. I imagine her trapped in a mirror instead. A permanent image of her locked into a rectangle of hard brightness, open-eyed.

When she left, she left her station wagon behind, and my father gave it to me when I got my driver's license. Now, driving it across town, I feel her beside me, giving directions, criticizing the landscape, the other drivers, the weather, which is a big fist of earth and sky with us struggling in it.

And I can hear her in the morning as I pour cereal into a bowl, telling me what's wrong with what I'm about to eat.

Now, at dinner, I sit in her chair at the dining room table, to get the view from there. My father looks handsome and boring across the table from where she'd be, and my own place shimmers with my absence instead of hers— dust motes, nothing. I try to imagine what she would have thought of Detective Scieziesciez, and remember the way she used to scoff at my father's weakness.

"You wimp," she said to him once when we were at Cedar Point Amusement Park and he wouldn't ride the Nile.

"I'll get wet," my father said.

"That's not what you're afraid of," she said, and he wouldn't look her in the eyes.

And I remember the way she watched Phil move around our house—his lanky teenage body, all breastbone, and the way his spine curved neatly into his jeans—like a woman with something on her mind. I could imagine the younger woman she once was looking back at the woman she'd become, thinking, This is where it's ended? All those long, sensual years spent slipping in and out of my body like an erotic pond or a fresh, white bed?

I was following my own flesh here?

I've sorted through the clothes in her closet for the skirts and sweaters that fit me, that I like, and I've taken over the expensive ones—the cashmere sweaters, the linen skirts. But the night before I wear them to school, I leave them in a pile on the bottom of my closet, to rumple them, so they no longer look like the clothes of someone's suburban mother. When they're dirty, I don't bother to dry-clean them. I just haul them to the basement, toss them from the washer to the dryer. They come out altered. Pilled, softer. I figure when she comes back, she can buy herself new clothes.

And some afternoons, when my father's gone, I lie on her side of the bed, the way I used to find her sometimes after school in mine, and I look at the ceiling that was hanging over my mother night after night.

"SO HOW DOES THAT FEEL?" DR. PHALER ASKS. "YOUR mother's been gone one year."

I shrug.

Dr. Phaler is lovely today in a white wool suit. The little silver spectacles perch happily on her nose. As always, her makeup is tasteful and soft. A rose-beige base. Basic red lips. Right now her eyelids are light blue, but she's done them well—not at all like *Charlie's Angels*, that bad seventies blue.

No. The light blue on Dr. Phaler's lids makes them shine like startling little pools, the kind you might glimpse from a jet over California. I want to be able to tell her how I feel about my mother being gone for one whole year, but what I say instead is what it seems a reasonable person in this situation would say she felt.

"Confused," I say. "Maybe mad."

Dr. Phaler looks disappointed. Perhaps she was hoping I'd cry. The one time I did cry in her office, I thought I noticed a swipe of red across her neck, as if she were excited. She whipped the box of tissues out so quickly I knew she'd been waiting a long time to do it. Those tissues were pink and clammy, and they smelled like a thin layer of lotioned skin when I blew my nose in them.

But I don't cry today. I don't feel sad—though I also don't feel confused, or particularly mad. I've only said these things because there are no adjectives for this lightness I feel, this *whiteness*. It's as though I've been caught in a diaphanous net—bodiless, that net holding my whole essence loosely in a breeze. Or as though I have weights around my wrists and ankles, but the weights are lighter than I am, as though I am wearing a dress made of emotion—a damp, invisible mesh. How could I possibly tell her that?

"After a whole year?" she asks, and I look down at my hands, which tremble a bit in my lap.

It was a beautiful year, I should add.

An early spring started one morning in March with a swarm of sudden, glassy, bird cries, and then the cool jewelry of primrose and violet loosened themselves in the dirt. Then summer burst into the world like a gorgeous car accident, opening eyes all over our bodies in the brilliant light. Fall—the smell of pumpkin guts, sluttish and unsweetened. Until winter fell all over us like pieces of heaven, glazed with oxygen or ether, hitting the ground in small, cold shards.

It was like a year in Eden where no Eve had ever lived.

WHEN I WAS A LITTLE GIRL, MY MOTHER TRIED TO CURL MY hair.

"Kat," she'd say after my bath, standing in the doorway as I toweled myself, steam obscuring us, as if we'd just stepped together into a Hollywood set of heaven, "let's do something with that hair."

In that heavenly Hollywood fog, perhaps we had wings.

I remember watching my own face in the mirror of her vanity as she rolled dark hanks of my hair into hot-pink cushions. I was maybe seven years old, and in that mirror the whole future was waiting for me like a skyline of cut-glass perfume bottles, silver tubes of lipstick.

She wanted me, as her female child, to be a sylph. A girl like a powder puff. Soulless, weightless, inhabiting the oxygen instead of the earth.

But I was awkward and overweight, with pin-straight hair—so much body on me I could never have lived in air.

And those nights of pink-cushion curlers worn to bed went on forever. I'd dream of Hansel and his older sister, Gretel, in a very dark forest dropping phosphorescent stones and bread crumbs behind them, hoping.

Those nights, knowing I'd wake without curls to my mother's disappointment, I couldn't roll over in bed because the curlers, tight as they were, would yank at my scalp. In my dreams I'd grab, panicked, for the fists of the witch who'd gotten hold of my hair, before I woke, remembering who and where I was and the curlers on my head.

Then, in the morning, she might even seem pleased. "Well, it's not curly, but it's *fuller*."

And briefly, she'd be right. The hair stood away from my head as if it were offended, but as the day wore on, it would settle down, and my mother would gaze across the dinner table with an annoyed expression on her face. She'd look at my father, and then at me again as we ate her turkey, like her silence, in thin, white slices.

"Pass the butter," my father would say.

With the butter in her hand, my mother would say, "*Please?*" holding it just out of his reach.

"Please?" he'd repeat. Without balls. Without imagination. A film of spit on his lower lip.

She could barely stand to eat in his presence.

I could tell by the look on her face that she wanted to throw her knife across the table and watch it vibrate in the wall. She might have been imagining the sound it would make, *boing*, as it wobbled there above my father's head.

By the time I asked for the butter, too, she would be seething.

"You don't need butter," she'd say, "you've got about twenty pounds of it on your hips."

"Evie," my father would say, looking down, counting the peas on his plate.

The first few times we'd tried to curl my hair, it had been her idea. But one night, maybe I was in fourth grade, the eve of picture day at school, when even the kindergarten girls of Garden Heights would be wearing pearls, pink sweaters, a little smudge of frosted lipstick, a swipe of powder on their noses and their mother's department store blush, I asked her to curl it for me, and my mother shrugged, looked at me as if she were sucking on something sour, and asked, "Why?" She said, "Your hair won't curl."

Bless my mother, I think some days, lying on her side of the bed, the bed she shared for twenty years with my father, looking at the ceiling, trying to imagine it from her perspective:

She was so *wicked*. Such a classic case of resentment and ambivalence bumping and brushing up against all that maternal instinct. The love and hate in her was as vast as space—all meteors, no atmosphere.

There she'd be, idling in the station wagon outside my elementary school, wearing a black turtleneck sweater and small gold hoops in her ears—beautiful and simmering. I'd come skipping out of the orange double doors with my book bag and braids looking like a daughter you might have in an ad, happy to see you, having learned the names of the continents that day. The bloated lung of Africa, the broken arm of Europe in a cast. Now, I could point those out. But, looking at me, my mother would seem to have forgotten who I was, why I was bounding into her car with some atrocity of crayon and construction paper in my hand with "for momy" written on it. She'd seem annoyed by my drooping kneesocks. Or a dry mustache of milk on my upper lip. As we drove home, she'd ask me about my day, but when I started to tell her about art or gym, she'd hush me, turn up the radio, while the announcer told her something she would rather hear, something about casualties and accidents and prisoners of war.

Still, there my mother would be—predictable, reliable—every afternoon, waiting for me. And in the morning, when she dropped me off, she'd hug me tight, kiss my hair three or four times, my cheek, the top of my head. "See you after school," she'd say, and look at me with sweetness like a sad song played on the radio so many times you couldn't hear the sadness anymore.

And every Christmas she'd bake fifty dozen of the most elaborate cookies you'd ever seen. Bells and doves and stars. Cookies shaped carefully into wreaths and candy canes, dough dyed green and red, with bows, with miniature poinsettias, the petals of which she'd clipped with little manicure scissors. Finnish chestnut fingers dipped in melted chocolate. Pfefferneusse. Cut-out cookies. Santas with glittering blue eyes, rosy cheeks, coconut beards. Christmas trees crowned with blonde and microscopic angels playing golden trumpets.

She had to use a magnifying glass to decorate their faces.

She had to use a skinny paintbrush dipped in colored egg white to shellac the trees with melted sugar so they glistened as if a fresh snow had just fallen on their branches.

Five dozen per batch.

Fifty dozen before she was done.

By June of every year, she'd have already made the dough, already have ten pounds of it wrapped in wax paper waiting in the freezer in the basement.

We'd gone through two freezers storing that. Years and years ago, the Ice-Master hummed itself to death in the basement. Then the Frigidaire. Now, the Coldspot.

We leave that Coldspot and its contents undisturbed. The dough in there belongs to my mother, and now the freezer is just a shelf collecting our lint and junk. A sock that's come out of the dryer, crackling with static, having mysteriously lost its mate. Bundles of old newspapers. My father has begun to move those from the basement floor, where they've been gathering for a decade, to the top of the freezer.

But for years my mother baked cookies out of that frozen dough, and those cookies made her the envy of the other mothers and their children. Plate after paper plate of her perfect perfection on display.

Still, she'd scowl at me as I ate those cookies.

"Jesus," she'd say as I bit into the sweet dust of an angel's wing, "you're getting fatter by the hour, Kat."

So, this was my mother. So?

We all had crappy childhoods. So?

And, of course, she never slapped me. We lived in a suburb without violence. My father didn't drink. He didn't even smoke. We had peace and money beyond the wildest dreams of 99 percent of the world—as much food as we could eat, as much Pepsi as we could drink. In the winter, we just turned the dial as high as we wanted and there was heat. We simply pressed a handle to flush our waste away. And water—as cold as we wanted, or as hot. What exactly did I want? How much more *plenty* could I have gotten?

Still, I used to lie in bed at night and imagine a huge, silent bomb detonating over our house, filling the air with a clean, poisonous gas that would get in my eyes and blind me, smell like bleach, kill us in our sleep.

My *hair*, I'd think in the morning as I passed the mirror in the hallway and caught a glimpse of my own light reflected in it, the refraction of a daughter she didn't want me to be, a daughter she had and had not wanted to have.

Where is she? I think now, passing that mirror, looking for myself.

Every night I pass that mirror on the way to my bedroom in the half dark of the hallway, and it looks like a cleft in the wall, a crack filled with dreams, tingling, star infested, a door to another dimension.

Where is she? I ask it, looking at me. And why did she leave?

"I'M NOT SURE," I SAY, AND DR. PHALER NODS. HER WOOL suit shimmers.

Dr. Phaler has clothes like moods. Passive, soft, pastel sweaters. Bitter navy blue suits and scarves decorated with geometric shapes, as sharp as words you've uttered and can't take back, words you have to wear, now, as a punishment around your neck.

She has a few premenstrual dresses, too—too tight, trying too hard to keep too much in, ready to let loose in an explosion of skin, popping the pearl buttons, ripping through the ribbons and lace—though Dr. Phaler is in her fifties. She must be done with blood. Or maybe not—

Once, I arrived twenty minutes early to my appointment and surprised her in the rest room in the hall outside her waiting room. She was wrapping something in tissue paper, and it looked like a tampon, or a newborn kitten— something bloody, with a tail. I might have gasped when I saw it in her hand.

"I'll be with you in twenty minutes," she'd said, professionally, throwing whatever it was into the trash.

But today she is a conservative bride, getting married at the courthouse in a hurry. But a bride with a secret, perhaps: Under her white skirt, I can see panty lines—a secret she's tried to suppress.

"I don't miss her," I continue.

Dr. Phaler bites her lower lip. "No." She shakes her head, and her blonde hair, which she's cut since I first came to see her about a year ago, clings in wisps to her eyes and lips. She whisks it away with her fingertips. "No, I didn't think you did."

Last January, Dr. Phaler would not have given me even this—this little hint that she knew who I was, suspected how I felt. In the beginning she only wanted to hear about my dreams—all those snowstorms I'd lost my mother in, all those locked trunks and frozen outhouses and buses skidding off the ice into ravines. Nodding, nodding, nodding.

That nodding, I must admit, gave me confidence. It was as if that nodding gave an order to everything, an A-okay: The Doctor has heard all this before, read it in a textbook, taken and passed a test on it.

That nodding made it seem as if those details, as random as they appeared, made some sense, added up to something for Dr. Phaler, accorded with her professional opinions, her scientific constructs, and I began to see a pattern in them myself—began to see the ways in which those blizzards represented my mother's distance, symbolized her emotional withholding, how her disapproval had become a metaphor in my dreams since she'd abandoned me for real, after so many years of cool remove, icy glances across the dining room table at my father and me—

And as I came to these conclusions, Dr. Phaler nodded.

Only once she said, "Your mother sounds cold-hearted," and then we *both* nodded in approval at how snugly all the pieces—the adjectives and the nouns and the experience and the dreams—fit: nodded at how simple the mind, in all its complexity, is. Perhaps we each pictured a heart, frozen in mid-beat, locked in a human ice chest.

It was at the end of one of those sessions, in the midst of one of these epiphanies, that I finally cried, and Dr. Phaler whipped out her box of sticky tissues—epidermal and pink.

But as the year spun forward, and I spent every Thursday from 4:00 to 4:50 in her office with its nearly empty bookcases and comfortable purple chairs, she started to ask for specifics. I told her how my mother, since I was a child, had told me I was fat, had not allowed me to put one morsel of food in my mouth without sneering at it—hexing, cursing, poisoning it—first. I told her how, in the weeks before she left, she'd begun to walk around the house half dressed, flirt with Phil, call me a pig in front of him—and Dr. Phaler, blue eyes darting around the room, pressed me for more. I told her about the night my mother came into my room and yanked the sheets off me, demanded to know if I was fucking Phil, called me a slut, and told me I was too fat and ugly to please a boy like that—and, finally, after all the hours of composure and nodding, nodding and composure, Dr. Phaler looked appalled and said, "What kind of mother would do a thing like that?"

It was her first judgment, and it stunned me.

Inexplicably, I felt something rush into my mouth—placenta, tentacles, phlegm—and, without missing a beat, I said, "*My* mother."

Of course, it had been rhetorical, and, answering that question, I sounded defensive, angry, all my naked longing and loss in those two words.

After that, at least once a session, Dr. Phaler asked that question, but I no longer answered.

Now, Dr. Phaler is braiding the silver chain from which her silver glasses dangle between her fingers. The fingers are elegant. The fingers of beautiful women—aren't they always like fancy cookies? *Lady fingers*.

I could imagine Dr. Phaler forty years ago, a little girl carrying a napkinful of cookies across the jade green of a lawn party in her own honor.

"No," she says, "I didn't expect you to say you *miss* your mother, but I do wonder how her absence for *one full year* might *make you feel.*"

I swallow. I say, "Surprised, I guess. I guess I'm surprised."

"What do you mean?"

"I mean, I guess I'm surprised she could hold out this long. I guess if nothing else I thought she'd come back for money, or shoes, or something else she needed."

"What about you?" Dr. Phaler sets those pale blue eyes on me. "Is it surprising that she could hold out this long on *you?*"

Now Dr. Phaler's glaring at the floor, at the face of my bad mother projected on her expensive oriental rug. She does not approve of my mother. She is paid to disapprove of my mother. It is what psychologists like her do for a living all day all over this country—express outrage at the failings of our mothers.

But why? Among some species, it's considered natural enough for a mother to gobble down her young—

A mother gets hungry.

A mother gets bored.

And who could blame her? As a baby, you were fat, and pukey, and dull. You knew only a handful of words, but she spent all day trying to talk to you. You clamped your mouth shut as she fed you, then knocked the spoon from her hands, laughed as it clanged across the floor. You shit your pants when she dressed you up, then screamed as she changed your clothes. You threw your shoe from the car window. You scratched your name in the paneling on the side of the station wagon.

"Do you love Mama?" she asked, and you shook your head *no, no, no.*

Not guilty by reason of insanity, any reasonable jury could conclude.

"Kat," she says, "I asked you a question. Aren't you surprised that she could hold out a whole year on *you*?"

Dear, beautiful Dr. Phaler—

Angel of Naiveté.

Angel of Stupid Questions.

For a year her predictability, her belief in the simplicity, the banality, of the human brain has thrilled and astounded and insulted me—

"No," I say, and shake my head. "It doesn't surprise me at all."

SHE'S WEARING A WHITE NIGHTGOWN, STANDING IN THE doorway of my bedroom. "Kat," she says, "I put my hands in the water, and they disappeared."

She holds her arms up, the sleeves of her nightgown slip down to the elbows, and I can see that the hands are gone.

"What water?" I want to know: I'm her daughter. I'm worried about my own hands.

"The dishwater," she says. "I was feeling the bottom of the sink for a spoon. The water was too cold."

I look at my fingers, which are longer than I remember them. They look fragile, and thin. From now on I'll be more careful, I think.

I look at my mother again.

There's no blood.

It's as if her wrists have sucked the hands into their sockets like something stared at too long, sealed up cleanly in two sealed eyes.

PHIL'S MOTHER SEARCHES THE ROOM WITH HER EAR, COCKING her head, moving it from side to side. "Do you hear that?" she asks.

"No," I say. "Hear what?"

"It sounds like scratching," she says, then makes the sound, "*Scratch, scratch, scratch.*"

"The furnace?" I offer, but she seems unconvinced.

"No," she says. "It's electrical. Like radio static. But regular. Rhythmical."

Phil looks annoyed: One good thing about having a blind mother is being able to roll your eyes right at her without getting slapped. Mrs. Hillman's face is pointed in his direction, but she can't see his expression—the boredom and total irritation with which he glares at her.

Still, I'm embarrassed for Mrs. Hillman. I look at her feet. Shoeless, in beige panty hose, they look a bit like Cornish hens, or fists—gnarled, with crooked, plucked wings. Her legs aren't long enough for those feet to touch the carpet as she sits back in my mother's stiff armchair, which also has stunted wings. She's a small woman, with drab curls. No makeup. She's wearing a housedress with big brown flowers on it—who ever saw a brown flower?— as if the garden's gone stale, all the roses overdone by sun or rusted in the rain, the gardener having long ago defaulted on his obligations.

Perhaps the salesgirls had a big, silent laugh behind the cash register as the blind lady bought that dress.

Mrs. Hillman is nothing like the other mothers in Garden Heights with their chunky gold jewelry, their designer slacks. She's nothing like *my* mother, who, despite her fondness for Phil, couldn't stand Mrs. Hillman.

"I know the new neighbors," I said one evening, trying to sound casual. Mrs. Lefkowsky, who'd lived next door to us all the years we'd lived in Garden Heights, had died. It was winter then, too, and a damp snow had begun to fall outside—big, white flakes in the pewter blue 5 P.M. sky. My mother was coming in from outside, and I could see that snow behind her when she opened the front door and stepped into the living room, a blanket of it covering Garden Heights with a camouflage of purity. Some of it was in her hair.

Next door, Mrs. Lefkowsky's porch light was on, but, of course, no one was home. She'd been dead for a month. The shades were pulled in each of her square windows, as if to separate the dark emptiness on the outside from the dark emptiness inside. Snow had buried her front steps, too—cloaked the roof in white corpse hair, and I remembered my mother's bitter adages about snow, quotations taken from her own mother:

The farmer's wife in heaven is plucking her white hen.

Or, *God is beating his angels again.*

I thought of our dead neighbor, Mrs. Lefkowsky, wearing a pair of skeletal wings in a frenetic afterlife. God going after her with his fists. A flurry of spine and feathers, which turned silver, then grizzled, as they hit the ground.

We hadn't liked her much, or thought about her often—Mrs. Lefkowsky. She was just the Daffodil Lady, the Widow Next Door. And then she died, and her daughter, along with her stubby husband, pulled up in a U-Haul and hauled her things away. My mother and I watched them from the kitchen window one Saturday afternoon. They were bundled in down jackets, stumbling across the front yard as they struggled with an olive green army trunk between them.

That trunk looked so heavy, I wondered what could possibly be in it. Salvaged bricks? Gold doubloons?

When that trunk slipped between them, it tore a gaping hole in the daughter's jacket, and a breath of feathers flew out. From the kitchen window it looked as if the daughter's body were a mattress full of fluff, hacked up. I could see her husband pick them out of his eyes, knock them out of his hair, spit them into the wind like a dry, choking snow.

My father was sitting in his La-Z-Boy with an ankle up on his knee, shaking his plaid slipper. "They're having some trouble over there," my mother said to him. "Maybe you should offer to help."

My mother had worried, after Mrs. Lefkowky's house was emptied out, that it might be sold to someone of poor quality, someone who might put plastic garden ornaments in the yard, someone with sticky children. So I was eager to give her the good news about Phil and his mother. She'd just come from the dentist, of whom she'd spoken highly for years, and often, and she was smiling.

Apparently, Dr. Heine was an attentive dentist. He polished my mother's teeth like miniature windows, gagging my mother pleasantly with his fat fingers, leaning over her in a silent and intimate embrace, mingling his minty breath with hers. When she opened her mouth wider, his white shoulder pressed into her neck. "Beautiful," he said, fingering her gums. "You must take good care of these babies."

My mother would swallow with her mouth open and try to smile, as if he were strangling her with her consent, with her blessing choking her to death. Then he'd hold a mirror up so she could see her teeth for herself, and she looked gorgeous in that mirror—flushed, lovely, dark hair subtly mussed, a bit disheveled. "See you in six months?"

Dr. Heine would ask, and there was a throaty touch of longing in his voice.

Once, after an appointment with him, my mother seemed so satisfied at dinner, sang Dr. Heine's praises so eloquently, that my father finally got up from the table and stomped up the stairs.

"Your father's jealous of my dentist," my mother said as if I hadn't noticed.

"So who are the new neighbors?" she asked, slipping her coat down her arms, feeling the coat closet for a hanger. The living room was brightly static with TV light, and, in it, I might have looked blue faced, drowned to her. I was still chubby. My hair was straight and brown, cut in a bit of a page boy. My eyes were blue: *good coloring*, at least. When and if I melted off some of that fat, I'd have that good coloring, and those good bones, which I got directly from her.

"Phil Hillman, and his mother," I said. "They're moving into Mrs. Lefkowsky's house. Phil is in my class. Phil Hillman."

"How do you know?" she asked.

"He told me today. He told me they bought the house next to ours."

"How did he know where you lived?" I could see it puzzled and bothered her that a boy knew where I lived. For years, she'd thought of herself as an ocean, and me as a small boat in it.

I shrugged. I said, "He said he saw me in the yard."

"Do you like him?" she asked, turning her back to me, hanging up the coat. "Not a thug or something?"

"He's great," I said. "I like him a lot." I paused. I wanted to say this gently, knowing what I knew about her, about what I meant to her. "He asked me out. Next Saturday. We're going to a dance."

My mother turned toward me again, and her mouth

swung open in a small hole of surprise, but she managed to turn it into a yawn. "Well, well," she said casually, indifferently. "Well," she said, as if she'd only half heard me, as if, after hours on a treadmill, she'd just stepped off.

My mother inhaled the little *o* with her yawn, then exhaled it over my shoulder, but her heart was beating hard. I could see that. I might as well have dragged her to the freezer by her hair, stuck her face right into it and made her breathe those rolling clouds of frost. In there, she might have seen her own face in a dentist's hands—a blurred plate, the features she was so pleased with dissolving as she stared.

My mother came over to where I sat on the couch, pushed the straight brown bangs off my forehead, ran a finger from my brow down to my chin, passed her thumb across my lips, which were an exact duplicate of her lips— but smoother, younger, sweeter. "Well," she said, "you're the girl next door now, I guess. Pretty romantic."

I shook my bangs back. "We'll see," I said. "It's just one date."

"Fat girls have to be pragmatic," I'd heard her say once about a cousin of my father's, a fat girl who'd married a crippled man. She'd said it as though she were talking about that cousin, but I knew she was talking about me.

Still, it was my first date, and I was her only child, her younger self, all she had, had ever had, was ever going to have—her life, going on without her, going out with a boy she hadn't met, to a dance she wouldn't be at, next to a movie she hadn't seen, and she might never see.

Already, she was starting to vanish.

I hadn't even gone on that date yet.

I was still fat.

I was still a virgin.

But my mother could already see what would happen next:

She pictured my twin bed with its starched sheets empty. She pictured me in a bridal gown. She pictured me in a supermarket pulling a child of my own by its fat arm past the fruits and vegetables. She pictured me in a white coffin wearing a lace dress, my face like a wax mask, and a delicate spray of baby's breath in my clenched fist.

But something wild was going on in that coffin. She looked closer. I was growing shoots and leaves and blossoms. Moss. Bugs. Worms. She leaned over my corpse to kiss my lips, but they were warm instead of cold, and then she realized the dead girl wasn't me at all. Who was that? Who was that dead girl squirming with life?

And then she realized—

That was her.

Our bodies had been switched. Mine for hers.

Perhaps she gasped when she saw that.

A FEW DAYS LATER, PHIL AND HIS MOTHER MOVED IN, AND my mother was the first person who went over to say hello.

"Welcome to the neighborhood," she said. "I'm Eve Connors. Next door."

A woman slipped her thin hand out the storm door, and the hand passed sleepily through the chill mist without direction. My mother had to catch it in midair. She pressed it into her own hand and felt it give—small-boned, with thin, cool skin. "I'm Gina Hillman." Then, "Come in."

There was a bit of humidity in the cold, a current of warmth running under it, and that current smelled like thawed water, old leaves, atomized ocean—as if a huge fan, pointed in our direction, had been turned on off the coast of Florida, and, by the time the wind kicked it up and billowed it to us here in our northeastern pool-table pocket of Ohio, it had accumulated the odors of the other states: the fish hatcheries, the sheep farms' eely wool, the stripped mountains and muddy football fields of Kentucky, the light blue haze of ditto fumes left over from the sixties that still hovered over hundreds of elementary schools between us— that chafed smell of paper, factory waste, the rheumy, old-lady smell of lace, dank and sweet, a fine drizzle of it in our faces. The telephone poles stood out stiff and black against the haze-white sky, like crucifixes minus Christs.

"I'm happy to meet you," Mrs. Hillman said, ushering my mother in.

My mother had never been in Mrs. Lefkowsky's house. It was oppressive. The ceiling was beige, and claustrophobically low. The carpet was worn away in patches, as if someone had stood in the same few spots, night after night for years, pawing at the ground like a horse for hours before moving on to another spot.

It was a shabby replica of our own house.

And the new neighbors had bad furniture, too, as bad as Mrs. Lefkowsky could possibly have had—scarlet curtains, vinyl lounge chairs, a coffee table as long as a coffin, with anchors adorning each end. There was even an afghan on the overstuffed sofa with an embroidered replica of the Liberty Bell.

My God, my mother might have thought, looking at that bell. It resembled an enormous breast, and the crack along the side of it was violent, sexual, sewn up sloppily with thick black thread. There was nothing on the walls, only old nails where Mrs. Lefkowsky must have had something hanging—her own *Seascape*, perhaps—until her greedy daughter and son-in-law carted it off.

There was no aesthetic here, no plan, no organizing principle at all. My mother must have been open-mouthed, looking around that house—my mother, who took such pains with our own house, her own aesthetic of polite denial, conservative grace. My mother, who was always so careful not to overdo anything, must have learned a lesson, in that moment, about what happens when you undo everything.

The decorator here, my mother thought, seemed to be denying the very *idea* of decoration.

The decorator here, my mother realized, must be blind.

"Welcome to the neighborhood," she said again into Mrs. Hillman's blank eyes, one of which traveled over my mother's face like a little, milky moon.

Mrs. Hillman gestured in the direction of the Liberty Bell as if my mother should sit near it, and when she sat, the sofa cushions surged around her like a warm plaid bath. Then Mrs. Hillman felt her way to the sofa herself, and eased back. Upstairs, someone could be heard—presumably Phil Hillman—singing in the shower. The sound of a young man's song—naked, muffled by falling water.

"Welcome, welcome," my mother said *yet again*—feeling absurd, struck dumb with discomfort.

"Thank you," Mrs. Hillman said and nodded. Her face was pointed in my mother's direction. "Can I get you a cup of coffee?"

"No," she said too quickly and looked at her hands. They were white. Though she'd only come from the house next door, she should have worn gloves, she thought. Or she shouldn't have come. "I hear you have a son," my mother offered, "the age of my daughter."

"Yes." Mrs. Hillman nodded blindly. "I hear they're going on a date."

They laughed.

Two mothers: One of whom, my mother thought—seized with a panic that felt like the fast snap of an elastic band on the delicate skin of a wrist—may never have glimpsed the face of her own child.

Mind you, my mother was never prejudiced against the handicapped. She did not think of them as possessed, or dangerous, or supernatural. She was not the kind of person who would look away from someone in a wheelchair. Instead, she'd look straight into his eyes and say hello, as if to let him know she was *not* superstitious, or ignorant. She did not think of herself as superior. She knew perfectly well it was only a matter of a few seconds in a station wagon on slick ice that kept her out of a chair just like it.

But, like everyone else, my mother carried a million fears with her wherever she went—phobias, trepidations, anxieties—most of them groundless, she supposed. Fables and old wives' tales.

Still, she carried them with her, as if in a tin—a pretty tin, the kind grandmothers keep beads and buttons in, a tin full of fish, stars, and trinkets.

And the blind were in it—along with bearded women, cancer, amputees—tapping their way across the intersection with their white canes, coming at her.

Ever notice how, if a blind man is headed in your direction, whichever way you try to escape, he will be headed that way?

Once, she'd had a blind teacher in elementary school. Mr. Ferguson. Music. The children in that class would pass notes to one another, make faces, put their heads down on their desks and sleep.

He was the first blind person my mother ever saw up close, and his face was badly shaved, pockmarked, pale. He wore dark glasses, but my mother could see that the eyes behind them were always open, as dispassionate and inorganic as Ping-Pong balls. His voice was frail and wavering, and when he sang he'd lift his chin toward the ceiling and sway sleepily—

My mother imagined him alone in his bed every night in the black, crooning like that to the silence, and she hated that picture. It was how she imagined death. Night closing down on you like a lid. No way out. Brightly, emptily white, or pure fluid darkness.

Perhaps my mother remembered this as she looked into Mrs. Hillman's eyes, then looked past her, around her house—the layout of which was identical to ours. Except for the smell of it, Mrs. Hillman might not know the difference between her own house and ours, and to think of that gave my mother a chill that began behind her knees—to imagine Mrs. Hillman in our home, to think that one day she might pull into our driveway and find Mrs. Hillman stumbling across our lawn, believing it was hers, or in our hallway. How was she to know where she was, or wasn't? My mother imagined Mrs. Hillman feeling her way to our bathroom, washing her hands in our sink, slipping into one of our beds without ever opening her eyes.

"Winter Formal," my mother said too cheerfully. "Yes. Tomorrow Kat and I are going to look for a dress."

Look—it echoed off the bare walls. She wished she'd used another word.

"Yes," Mrs. Hillman nodded. "Phil's renting a tux."

"Kat's excited," my mother said.

"So is Phil."

Mrs. Hillman's chin drifted toward the kitchen, and my mother looked in that direction, too. There was the sound of footsteps overhead, a door opening.

First, my mother saw his legs, in jeans. The big brass buckle of his belt, and then the skin of his stomach, and the sparse, damp hair on his chest, between his nipples—those hard, dark buttons of flesh. She could see his ribs—he was boyishly thin—how they tapered into his waist as if a witch's bony fingers had grabbed him from behind, as if the witch were squeezing him. His face was long, shaved. Dark eyebrows. But his hair was light—the straw blond of a child—and it was wet, combed back. When he saw my mother, he said, "Oh."

"Phil," Mrs. Hillman said without turning in his direction, still speaking to the kitchen, "this is Kat's mother. Mrs. Connors. Our new neighbor."

"I'm sorry," Phil said, covering his bare stomach with his arms. "I heard something. I didn't know anyone was over. Nice to meet you, Mrs. Connors." And he hurried back upstairs.

There was a hollow place in his back where his spine swerved neatly into his jeans.

PHIL AND HIS MOTHER ARE AT OUR HOUSE THIS AFTERNOON because their basement flooded last night, and now the plumbers and the forty-dollar-an-hour workers have come to patch and bail. They're pounding in and out of the house in their big boots with the doors wide open on a ten-degree winter afternoon.

Last night, while Mrs. Hillman was bathing—hot water and bubbles spilling over her—she'd heard the rush of bursting pipes, the gulping ocean roar of plumbing run amok. "Phil!" she'd shouted, feeling her way out of the tub, both hands gripping the slick rim.

Phil pretended not to hear her at first. He thought she just wanted something, like a sponge, or that she'd dropped her washcloth, or she'd slipped, or she couldn't find her bathrobe because it had fallen off the hook, and he couldn't bear to walk into the bathroom, to see his mother's long breasts naked, to see her soaped and groping toward him with her needs, her panic disguised as impatience—

"Where were you?" she'd want to know. "I've been shouting for ten minutes."

But then he'd heard the basement overflowing, too. Water, he told me on the phone a few hours later, sounds just like fire, and his first thought was that the house had burst into flames, that he'd have to haul his mother out into the snow without her clothes, that she'd catch pneumonia and die—or worse, that she would suffer for a very long time, complaining.

Now Mrs. Hillman is cocking her head in our living room again—a mechanical Mrs. Claus in a Christmas department store display. Phil bounces his foot nervously, ankle on his knee, glaring at his mother. He looks rangy in a flannel shirt this afternoon, thermal underwear beneath it, like a blond boy playing the part of a woodcutter in the high school play.

She listens. Fogged eyes wide.

"It's nothing, Mother," Phil suggests. "It's probably the furnace, like Kat says."

"Do you want some more coffee?" I ask politely, trying to make up for Phil's unkindness—his tone, which is the tone of an angry youth, a disrespectful son, one who needs a father around to frighten him now and then.

"No," Mrs. Hillman says, fidgeting with the rim of her empty cup, looking worried.

"Maybe it's my father," I offer. He's upstairs, and won't be coming down as long as Phil is here. Although my father admires Mrs. Hillman—her spunk, her homely courage ("She's a good woman," he says. "The kind of woman you could hang your hat on if you had to")—he refuses to come into any room Phil's in. This has gone on for more than a year now, since before my mother left, since the afternoon he caught me with him in my bed,

Phil's naked ass rising and falling over the pale shadow of my body.

It had been an accident. Until then, Phil and my father had gotten along well—nervous and polite in each other's company, chatting about football, looking respectfully at the emptiness just beyond each other's shoulders as they shrugged and nodded.

But my father had come home from the boat show in Toledo early. "Daddy," I'd called to his back as he hurried down the hall. "It was my idea." But he didn't turn around. I could hear water running in the bathroom sink behind the closed door for over an hour.

"I'll look around," I say in Mrs. Hillman's direction, "if that will make you feel better."

"I'm sure I hear something," she says, which means she wants me to look around.

Phil's hands turn into fists, as if he's just grabbed two slim throats in them. Maybe he hates her, and who could blame him? It would be nearly impossible to be her son. Her stubbornness. Her needs. "What will I ever do?" Phil asked me angrily one afternoon as we drove together to the grocery store on some errand his mother had sent us to do. "I can't ever leave, now that my father has. She can't even open a can."

"Oh, Phil," I said, "you're her son, not her father. She has to let you go."

"No, she doesn't," he said, and I could see a blue vein in his temple. I didn't want to think about whether or not what he said was true, but I could see how hard it would be for him to imagine the rest of his life, and where it would lead him, unless she died. It would be like having a job in a fortune cookie factory, standing all day on an assembly line while optimism passed through your hands on flimsy strips of paper—"You will inherit a million dollars," "You will go on an exotic vacation"—but never moving, standing in one place while the damp batter of the fortune cookies slid by, all your possible futures settling into that clamminess as it passed.

Once, I looked out my bedroom window and saw Phil in the backyard with his mother, a plastic basket full of laundry between them. She was telling him how to hang it on a line, and the wet sheets looked as heavy and limp as dead women. I could see she was worried that he'd drop the clean laundry on the ground. She was gesturing, tugging on his arm, until finally a pair of her underpants slipped out of his hands, dropped at his feet. Phil just left them there for a while, and then he stepped on them, hard, purposefully, before hanging them on the line—white, over-bleached, too intimate, and dirty.

I hated seeing that laundry hanging in their backyard.

But then it started to rain, and Mrs. Hillman made him take it all down and bring it in again.

Mrs. Hillman is dogged, obstinate, a woman like a log. Perhaps she has to be, being blind. If she didn't insist on the correctness of her perceptions of every single thing, who would ever believe her perceptions, ever, of anything?

"She drove my father to the edge," Phil said once, and I pictured Mr. Hillman in the passenger seat next to his blind wife, screaming, hands over his eyes while she drove ninety miles an hour through football fields and forests and backyards strung with laundry flapping on their lines until somehow, miraculously, she slammed on the brakes just before they hit the edge, the place where the world ends, the crater into which Mr. Hillman had flown— through the windshield, smashing through the glass, a sparkling, bloody husband disappearing into the abyss.

For fifteen bright, white years like wet sheets they were married, and had been since high school, when Phil's father first fell in love with Mrs. Hillman after glimpsing her inside the special ed classroom where she spent her days. An exotic mushroom—something that only grew, all waxy flesh and pale meat, in the light of the moon. He watched her from a distance and must have thought for a long time about what it would be like to kiss a blind girl, to take her clothes off in the dark backseat of his car. Like a goat sneaking up on a milkmaid. Or a bear carrying a virgin into the forest. There was something dirty about it, but everyone would think of you as good for doing what you did, because you loved a girl no one else would want.

But after a decade of that, Mr. Hillman decided his whole life had been a correctable mistake, decided that, since Phil was old enough to take care of Mrs. Hillman, he could leave, become a drifter—a drifter with quite a bit of money, as it happened, as the job he left when he abandoned Phil and his mother was a good one, and he'd been saving money a long time and investing it wisely with drifting in mind.

After that, Phil and his mother left their executive home for Garden Heights, for the expired Mrs. Lefkowsky's house—a junior executive, which wasn't squalid, of course, but was not the kind of house they'd moved out of.

Once, early after we'd first started dating, Phil drove me past that house in High Hollow Estates.

"That one," Phil said, pointing to a huge brick facade. Inside, I could see a black woman moving from room to room. She seemed to be cleaning the air with a rag. "I grew up there," Phil said, pulling into the driveway, then backing out. "That woman used to be ours."

A fairy tale with a twisted ending, one in which the sun sets like napalm on the prince and princess as they walk off, sticky all over with fire.

When I come back from the kitchen Mrs. Hillman says, "Look upstairs. Right above us. It sounds like a squirrel burrowing."

"For Christ's sake," Phil says, standing up. "Just sit down, Kat. There's no squirrels anywhere except in my mother's head."

"Phil," I look at him with my eyes wide, knowing his mother won't notice, "it can't hurt to check. It's probably just my father."

But it's not. My father's asleep on his back on the bed. He's wearing a sweatshirt that says "U.M." in big blue letters, like a hesitation on his chest.

LATER PHIL SAYS, "YOU JUST DON'T GET IT. YOU DON'T have to live with her."

We're on our way to the Rite Aid in his father's car to buy the can of air freshener his mother wants. "Glade," she'd said back at the house after the workmen were gone, "floral." She handed her pocketbook to Phil and said, "I can smell them in here. Sewage and boots. Take three dollars."

Phil took an extra ten out of her wallet and slipped it into his.

"I know," I said, watching the road roll out its rug of slush in front of us. It's gotten warmer: the usual big January thaw making its annual two-day appearance, duping us into thinking winter's nearly over when, really, it's just begun. "But she deserves to be treated with respect, Phil. She can't help it that she's blind."

He glances at me, and the car veers a little closer to the curb. His face is scrunched up, eyes narrowed. I look away, back at the curb, which is painted yellow. A warning.

When I look back, he's glaring at me. He says, "Do you think I don't know that?"

Something flutters under my arm then. As if I've got a little mouse hidden under it. An artery, pumping. I realize I'm scared. "Forget it," I whisper into the windshield. "I'm sorry I said anything."

"Do you think I don't fucking know that it's not her fault she's blind?"

I shake my head. "Of course not," I say. "I just felt bad for her today."

"Well." Phil looks back at the road now, slowing, turning, seeming satisfied. "Well, a person could spend his whole life wandering around looking for things my mother thinks she hears and smells all over the goddamn house. Ten times a day she's asking me, 'Do you smell something moldy? Phil, go look in the attic, I think I hear a bat.'" He imitates his mother's voice—whiny, childlike, but hard-edged, a cross between Betty Boop and my own mother, whose voice, I realize, I've nearly forgotten until now, hearing a bit of it in Phil's impression.

I shrug. "It didn't hurt me any just to check around the house. I don't see what difference it makes to you. She was right last night, wasn't she? About the plumbing?"

"So what?" Phil stops the car in the Rite Aid parking lot, squeezing between two fat mini vans. "*So fucking what?*" he asks again, slamming the car door, hurrying toward the store.

I unbuckle my seat belt, open the car door, and step into the parking lot, which is glazed with ice that's been thawing and freezing and thawing now for two months, and I try to hurry after him, but, under me, the parking lot is slick, shifting in panes of gray beneath my boots, and I start to skid. Slipping, I see the fogginess of that slush rush at me, as if I've stepped into the path of a nebulous mirror. "Phil," I call out, and for an instant I glimpse my own surprised face in that mirror as I fall among the swirling clouds and slop—

In that reflection, I'm wearing a veil of slop. The pavement underneath it stings the heel of my hands, and the hot pain brings tears to my eyes.

"Are you all right?" he asks, turning around, finding me behind him on my hands and knees, looking up, seeming to cry. He comes over but doesn't reach down to touch me, just hovers, casting a wan shadow. I sit, now, resigned, and the slop starts to seep up through my jeans. I feel it spread through my panties, onto my bare skin, and the tears feel hot, the way it feels to pee after swimming in ice-cold water, the way freezing begins as cold and ends as burning.

"HOW ARE THINGS WITH PHIL?" DR. PHALER ASKS TEN minutes before my hour's up. By now, we have entirely dispensed with the pretense of psychoanalysis, the pretense that there is something scientific or medical about these hours we spend together. We no longer sift through the details of my childhood and dreams for trouble. That laborious process bore no fruit—just some dull nuggets, like unsalted cashews: a string of images that were not symbols, memories of childhood birthday parties at which no fun was had, insults endured in elementary school rest rooms. Even the subject of my mother has been for the most part exhausted, except on special occasions, like her birthday or my parents' anniversary. Instead, we spend my sessions mulling over the trivia of the present, its minor annoyances and daily travails.

It is like gossiping once a week with a friend, except that the gossip is about me.

And, for a hundred dollars an hour, Dr. Phaler is a good dispenser of lightweight advice. She never seems distracted. She monitors her facial expressions for just the right display of detachment and compassion, and she always remembers the names of the minor characters in my life—my chemistry teacher, my friends Beth and Mickey, the assistant principal who caught me smoking in the parking lot and gave me a warning.

Dr. Phaler is like the mother you always wished you had. The mother you would have been perfectly happy to pay a hundred dollars an hour to have. Except that you could never afford such a mother. If you had to *buy* a mother, you'd end up with some old lady who lived with a dozen other kids in a trailer. Or a mother who'd get sick of you and leave, like the one I had.

"Not good," I say. "I don't get it."

"What don't you get?"

"Well," I say, and look up at the ceiling of her office, which is tiled with white boards. The boards look porous, false, too light to be a ceiling, as if they've been pressed from dust and the buoyant, brittle hair of old ladies, as if they'd fly away if someone sneezed, leaving us roofless, exposed to the sky.

"He says he loves me, but we just don't have anything together anymore. We don't talk. We don't hold hands. When I try to kiss him, he gets rigid," and I see myself up there on the ceiling, projected onto those white tiles as on a drive-in movie screen, kissing Phil, Phil standing up straighter, backing away, as if I am an overly affectionate dog, one that might turn out to be vicious.

"What does he say when you ask about this?"

"He says he's got a lot on his mind right now. To cut him some slacks. I think he means slack—"

Dr. Phaler laughs. She is familiar by now with this aspect of Phil's character, his struggle to express himself in clichés, never quite getting the cliché right, and it is a joke between us.

"He says kissing just doesn't do anything for him. He feels numb inside. He complains about his mother a lot, says she's ruining his life with her whining, that he needs some space."

"Do you think about ending the relationship?" Dr. Phaler asks, sounding serious, though she is still smiling at our joke.

"For what?" I ask, looking down from the ceiling tile and back at Dr. Phaler.

"Do you mean *what for?*"

"No." I shrug. "I mean *for what?* There aren't any other boys to date around here—dorks and jocks. I don't want one of those. And I don't have a real active social calendar right now. It's not like Phil's standing in the way of some glamorous alternative lifestyle I might be leading."

"So?" Dr. Phaler is playing the fool. "Do you have to stay in a relationship that's unsatisfactory because no other relationship is available? Wouldn't you be better off with no boyfriend at all than with one who doesn't even want to express affection? Kat," she leans toward me in her chair, looking hard into my eyes, "isn't that a lot like the relationship you've described your parents as having? Haven't you always said your mother married your father because there was no one else around to marry? Kat," she continues, glancing at the clock, which is about to run out, "I want you to spend some time this week thinking about your parents' marriage. Can you do that?"

I don't bother to answer. Of course, of course. So many connections to be made. So many obvious parallels. Do we really need a Ph.D. for this?

Besides, my time is up.

It occurs to me to tell Dr. Phaler about my fantasies

concerning Detective Sciezesciez, how it has crossed my mind that I could make an appointment with him on the pretense that I need to discuss the case of my missing mother, and that this appointment might end with my legs spread on this detective's desk.

But Dr. Phaler looks satisfied, as if she's given me a tidy box of explosives to carry with me onto the plane. She stands and opens her door to usher me out, and she smiles sympathetically but says nothing more than "See you next week" as I step out of her office, smile my good-bye politely.

Leaving, I see a young woman, maybe twenty-one, sitting in the waiting room, waiting for Dr. Phaler. This is the third or fourth time I've seen her there—as pale and thin as an exhalation. She looks a little shaky, and smells like smoke doused with watery perfume. Bulimic, I imagine: At our high school we have quite a few of those, and I recognize the type. This one looks like a woman perfectly capable of going home and eating four gallons of vanilla ice cream with a big, silver spoon—like eating pleasure itself: creamed, sweetened, frozen, momentary. Then gagging it back into the toilet, washing her face in the sink, rinsing out her mouth, then going straight back into the kitchen for a bag of potato chips—

Those chips would be painful, though.

So many golden sections.

Coming up again, it might feel as though idealism itself had gotten caught in your throat. But it could be satisfying, too. A hard job well done, choking perfection back into the world outside yourself.

Today the bulimic has on too much lipstick, smeared all over her lips as well as above and below them. She glances up from her fashion magazine at me, and her forehead looks cool and damp. And those lips: It looks as if she's been kissing something painted red while the paint's still wet, or as if she's just come back from an emergency room, where she kissed someone bloody.

When she smiles at me, I see the shape of my own smile cut itself into the clamminess of her brow, and I imagine she can see some distorted reflection of herself somewhere on me.

THREE

JANUARY 1988

THE GRANDMOTHERS CAME FOR CHRISTMAS, AND ALTHOUGH it's been a month since they left, I still feel as though I might turn any corner in the house and find one of the grandmothers there—wolf mouth open, arms outstretched, ready to eat me alive.

My mother's mother, Zeena, and my father's mother, Marilyn, are crazy about each other. Every morning of their long visit, there they'd be when I came downstairs, sitting on the couch, knees pressed together, hands in a huddle between them, discussing my mother's disappearance in whispers, marveling at how terribly and well she's vanished.

Two years. Almost two years.

Grandma Zeena is thin, hard, robust. She looks every inch the woman who, decades ago, left her only child behind in Ohio, moved to the desert, started a bright new life, and didn't look back. My mother kept a snapshot of Zeena pinned to the mirror over her dresser, and it's still there. Like everything else, my mother left it when she left us.

In that photograph, Zeena's standing to the left of a roulette wheel, smiling. The wheel is wild with numbers and lights, rhinestones and gold letters, and Zeena is getting ready to spin it. The expression on her face is wide open, the face of a clock without hands—free of liability, or fear. Whatever happens, this photograph implies, she'll still be smiling—not smugly, but with true, untroubled joy.

Perhaps Zeena sent this particular snapshot back to her daughter in Ohio as a kind of apology—one that tried to express how we live, really, at the mercy of chance, the accidents of our own impulses, the toss-up of our individual desires. And now that my own mother has left, I think maybe all those hours she spent at the mirror, fussing and unfussing, buttoning and unbuttoning, putting earrings on and taking them off, she kept that photo of Zeena as a model there beside her own reflection, beside the image she was making of herself.

Grandma Zeena managed to go a decade without seeing her daughter. "Time just flew by," I heard her say one Christmas to my mother. Zeena had flown in for the holiday then, just as she did this year, and the two of them were in the kitchen, peeling potatoes at the sink. I looked at those two women holding blunt roots in their hands, those women I'd issued directly from, and pictured Time as a mechanical sparrow with a little clock radio in its belly, whizzing back and forth between them.

When my mother finally flew at the end of that decade to Las Vegas, at the age of twenty, Zeena met her, according to my mother, with a plastic bag of gifts—a teddy bear, a charm bracelet—as if she were expecting the child she'd left in Ohio to step off that plane, unchanged, ten years later. My mother said she thought Zeena seemed a bit suspicious when she tapped her shoulder and said, "Mom, it's me."

"Who?" Zeena asked, the sound of coins slapping slot machines in the airport lobby—tinny, mechanical music.

Later, over margaritas in a casino, sitting at the bar while more machines whirred wildly behind them—nickels, wheels, whistles—Zeena told my mother that she'd never loved my mother's father, that it was why she left. My grandmother's eyes were aquamarine in the salt light of her margarita, the color of a couple of rhinestones dropped out of a showgirl's tiara into dust.

She continued, "I was pregnant, you know. Kicked out of the house. Too young to know what else to do." As she spoke, Zeena chewed a ragged fingernail, painted red—and, replaying the moment in her mind for many years, my mother would think of that hangnail as a bloody claw caught in her mother's mouth. An owl's claw, or a fish-hook: Her mother had stuck it in her mouth herself, but she seemed snagged by it, helpless, there in Las Vegas.

"How *is* your father?" she asked, and before my mother could answer, Zeena added, "Now *there's* a man who knows *nothing* about women."

My mother never had a chance to answer because they had to hurry. Zeena's new boyfriend, Roger, was picking them up outside the Lady Luck in his new convertible. They were going to show her the sights. "Bottoms up," Zeena said, tipping her glass toward my mother's, "time to fly."

That last sip of margarita might have tasted like a man's sweat in my mother's mouth, and she felt nauseated, spongy. The Friday before, she'd graduated from college, and that afternoon she'd flown across the country. Zeena had sent her the ticket slipped into a card that said "con-gratulations" inside, but on the outside was a drawing of a couple kissing, not a diploma or a graduation cap, and when her father dropped her off at the airport he said, "Now don't give her any money. She said this was a gift."

It was the first plane ride of my mother's life, and looking down on the country slipping under her like something spilled had made her sick. And as soon as she and Zeena stepped together out of the air-conditioned airport, the heat hit her with the weight of a burning wall, and Zeena said, "You know, I'll have to borrow some money to pay a cab to get us back to the apartment. I spent every last dime on that plane ticket, Eve." My mother fished around in her purse, and handed her mother twenty dollars. It was one hundred degrees out there in the blank heat of the desert under a flat, colorless sky. As they waited for a cab on the sidewalk, my mother couldn't stand on both feet for very long, the concrete boiling under the flimsy soles of her sandals. She had to keep switching feet as each one got too hot, and she felt like a bird in her white sundress—a big white chicken stranded in the desert, dancing on sand.

My mother told this story right in front of Zeena at Christmas dinner that year, and as she told it, Zeena laughed. She wore that same unapologetic expression she wore in the snapshot with the roulette wheel.

Even now, Zeena's hair is blonde. She wears pencil-shaped skirts and thin knit sweaters, push-up bras. Her body is oddly solid, muscled—not like a young woman's, but like a statue's—though her face looks every year of her sixty-seven, half of them lived beneath a merciless Nevada sun, washing the sky with toxic light.

But her teeth are narrow and sharp. They are the teeth of a woman who could chew up carpet tacks and spit them out all over the house. It's no wonder, I think, looking at her, that my mother was the kind of mother she was.

"Kat," she asked me on Christmas Eve, sitting on the edge of my bed, leaning into me, "do you know where your mother is?"

"Grandma," I said, sincerely shocked and sounding it, "do you think if I knew I wouldn't tell you?"

Zeena swallowed that, and it looked like a spoonful of splinters going down.

"I guess you would," Zeena said. Then she thought. "But your mother was a secretive girl. I suppose you could be, too. You know," she looked down at her fingernails, which were long and painted mother-of-pearl, "that Detective What's-his-*shh* called me again a few weeks ago to ask if I'd heard from Eve."

"And?" I asked.

"And I told him, I said, 'Pal, you might as well just close the case on this one. Hell will freeze over before that woman comes back. She's my daughter, and she's got running in her blood.' "

I swallowed.

I thought of Detective Scieziesciez's back, his trench coat. Sometimes at night I'd still think of him. His rough face pressed between my legs. I'd imagine him pulling up in his dark car, as he did that one day, busting through the front door of our suburban home with his gun drawn, sweeping me up in his arms, throwing the frilly bedspread to the floor in one clean sweep. "Everything here looks perfectly normal," he'd say, as he'd said then, but this time he'd be yanking my panties down to my knees as he said it.

I was hoping I'd get to see Detective Scieziesciez again at least once before he closed my mother's case, and I hoped my grandmother hadn't said anything to make the chances of that any slimmer than they already seemed.

Marilyn appeared in the doorway then, a red dressing gown loose and frilled around her ample hips and the big, generous, water balloons of her breasts, blocking the light from the hall. Unlike Zeena, Marilyn is soft—a garden of petunias after a long, hard, humid rain. Her hair is red. ("Not just dyed," my father would say, "that hair is dead.") She has been a widow longer than she was married, and loves everyone to distraction. Over and over she'll say, "I love you," or "I *loved* him," eyes tearing up, "I just loved the *hell* out of your grandpa Sam"—who'd died one day of a stroke while Marilyn was frying pork cutlets, just dropped over on the kitchen floor as though someone had snuck up behind him and pulled a drawstring too tight around his neck—or, "I loved the stuffings out of every one of my sons." By the time she's done, you are embarrassed about how few and little you've loved, how stingy you've been with your affections.

"You're *so* much like your mother," Marilyn said. "It's uncanny. The resemblance. It gives me the chills. I just *loved* your mother."

She shuddered, to show us.

Outside, there was the sound of humming—power lines, or jets, or Santas cruising over us in their electric sleds.

THE PHONE RINGS IN THE MORNING AS I'M GETTING READY for school, pulling black tights up to my waist, doing a little dance in the bathroom to get them on.

Before I lost weight, I'd wear whatever was clean in my closet, whatever I could squeeze into, whatever I imagined my mother would not complain too much about when I emerged from my bedroom into her line of vision ("Jesus, Kat, you're not going to wear *that*?").

But since I've been thin, dressing myself in the morning has gotten harder. The night before, I lie in bed and imagine myself in various combinations of skirt and sweater, and then in the various poses I might be seen in wearing them—leaning over the drinking fountain in the hall at school, slurping that water the temperature of body fluids, a tepid stream of something human and nauseating in my mouth. Or sitting behind my desk in Great Books, legs crossed at the ankles while Mr. Norman drones on and on about *Paradise Lost*.

Mr. Norman wears horn-rimmed glasses and weighs only about a hundred pounds, but his lectures make Satan seem sexy and slick, like someone Mr. Norman himself might secretly admire.

Listening, I imagine Satan and Detective Scieziesciez

waiting for me in a silver Thunderbird in the high school parking lot, smoking cigarettes, waiting to see what I'm wearing that afternoon.

God knows there's no one else at my high school to dress up for, no one who matters, no one who would look at me twice even if I walked down that gray corridor stark naked. Phil wouldn't notice, and my closest friends, Mickey and Beth, aren't exactly fashion plates themselves. At Theophilus Reese High, by twelfth grade, you are whoever you've been until then. Your lot's cast early. Your lot. Your caste.

And, back when it mattered, back when the beautiful kids had been sorted from the homely, I'd been fat. Now, no matter what I weigh, until graduation day, I will be Fat.

But lately I've noticed men—some of them older than my father—watching me walk in and out of restaurants, watching me walk from my mother's station wagon, which is mine now, into McDonald's, or the library, or the mall. "Is this yours?" a man in an expensive black suit asked me one afternoon last week as I stood in line at the drugstore with a package of tampons. He was out of breath and holding a limp red mitten in his hand. I shook my head, looking at it. That bloody hand, extended.

"Oh," he seemed disappointed, and then chagrined. "Well, then, would you like me to buy you a sandwich somewhere?"

It was pathetic, and we both laughed. I handed the cashier my tampons, and even she looked shy. "I can't," I said.

He looked at me for a few seconds before he said, "You're an awfully attractive woman," and then he left, winking over his shoulder as the automatic doors jolted open nervously for him, and the cashier stuffed my package into a plastic sack. "Some men..." she said, but she wouldn't look me in the eyes.

He'd only been gone a moment before I'd forgotten

what he looked like, or why I hadn't wanted the sandwich he wanted to buy.

Being noticed is new, and every day I have to prove to myself it can be done again to believe it ever has. In my imagination every night, I pan around the room I will be in the next day like a little Tinkerbell, viewing myself from every angle, appraising myself from the front, the back, above, below—a whirring electric eye.

Of course, by morning I'm afraid to wear anything at all, and it takes hours to get ready for school. By the time I'm done, there's a stripped heap of clothing on the bedroom or bathroom floors, as if the girls who'd been wearing those outfits had dissolved, sweaters and skirts dropping out of the air where they'd been.

A lot of trouble. For what?

But in the morning, at our lockers, outside the vinegar glare of the gym, Beth says, "You look great, Kat. I like your sweater." Of course, it wouldn't matter what I was wearing, or how I looked in it, Beth would say that: It is Beth's role. Like an usher in an auditorium, handing out programs, saying, "Enjoy the show," Beth is there for me. Even when I am bitter, or premenstrual—cramped, depressed, snapping at Beth—she will tell me I look good, smell good, did the right thing.

Still, I can tell when she really means it, and lately she really means it. Lately, everything I wear looks right. The janitor calls me, "Hey, kitty-cat," purring as he moves his mop around and around on the floor.

"He's got the hots for you," Beth says, gesturing at the janitor, who has a limp, who has the name, or the word, "Dick," embroidered above his heart.

I've known Beth since third grade, since she and I were fat girls together standing in the snow at recess, watching the other girls jump rope. We were both too fat to be invited to join them, so after a while we had to talk to each other. Those girls would jump faster and faster in a blur of limbs and clothesline while we waited in our big rubber boots for the bell to ring and call us back into the warmth of Mrs. Mulder's classroom.

Finally, out of sheer boredom, we invented a game of our own, which had to do with the teeter-totter. We'd go up and down, up and down, chatting amiably, but then one of us, the one who was down, would casually slip off the end and let the other one, the one who was up, crash back to earth.

The object of this game was to slide off your end of the teeter-totter when the other least expected you to—perhaps in midsentence, smiling—in order to heighten the terror and thrill of suddenly plummeting through air, pure gravity, a fat girl with wings shot out of the sky.

The first time Phil and I had sex, I remembered that game with Beth. The jovial anticipation of danger and pain, looking all the time into her inscrutable face as she looked into mine.

Although I've lost thirty pounds, Beth stubbornly remains sixty pounds overweight. She has become a bit of a celebrity at school—admired, but not liked: an object of envious pity. Beth's claim to fame is the steel trap of her brain. She's won every math award the state of Ohio has to offer, and her bedroom walls are papered with certificates and plaques and letters of congratulation signed by one of the governor's aides. Even when she's simply eating a fruit pie in the cafeteria, that brain is chewing up the computable world and its reams of ticker tape.

"Kat," she said to me once when I told her how many pounds I'd lost, "that's 489 ounces. 32.7 milligrams. 457 liters of fat," or something like that.

"Jesus Christ, Beth," I said, "shut up. I don't want to know that. What makes you think people want to know stuff like that?"

I sounded like my mother as I said it.

Beth looked sad, with her bland face, her light brown hair. It is the same face she wore long ago, back on the teeter-totter. Little girl pudginess. A bit desperate, painfully clever, and stuffed up with secret rage.

The third of us is Mickey.

"The weird sisters," my mother used to call us, or "the three blind mice."

Like me, Mickey's lost weight, left the fat-faced girl we met in seventh grade behind her like a bad date, ditched. She's a cheerleader now, having snagged one of those coveted positions with all its myth and pomp and prestige despite being unpopular and acne-scarred.

Though they must not have wanted to give it to a girl like Mickey, the selection committee simply could not have denied her a place on that squad. Even Miss Beck, the cheerleading coach, with her perky smile and high cheekbones, all cream and peaches, must have had to admit that Mickey *is* cheer, pep, the fighting spirit of pride—the personification of it.

"The Savages" our teams are called. Mickey's job is to urge them on.

But, according to Mickey, the other girls on the squad won't even sit next to her on the bus as it lurches and wallows its way across Ohio for our team's away games. That bus, Mickey says, smells like panties.

FDS. Scent: Spring Rain.

As if a cool May afternoon were clamped between those cheerleaders' legs, its sweet mist rising from their crotches, condensing on the windows of the bus.

Those pretty things will not, apparently, accept Mickey as one of them. Instead, they huddle together, swapping a hairbrush that grows more and more beautiful with silk and gold as it passes.

But, as I've said, Mickey could inject team spirit into the heart of a dead man—cartwheeling, scissoring, frantic zeal. Dancing to the flat music of the pep band, she is a morale machine. Arms and legs and voice, the tilt of her head, the sway of her hips, synchronized. More than once, Beth and I have sat together in the brisk wind of a football game and watched our friend go wild with blood lust on the field, leaping, backlit by the pure glare of stadium light and scoreboard neon—"*Ho ho, hey hey, we are going to make you pay*"—and shaken our heads in admiring disbelief. After a close game, Mickey might be hoarse, or even voiceless, for days.

But the acne scars along her jawline and on her chin sometimes burn purple beneath the skin—angry, permanent scars, seething, rising to the surface on damp days, especially in the harsh light of late winter or early spring. I never knew Mickey when she had acne, though I've know Mickey for what seems like forever, and she's always had those scars. Perhaps she was born scarred.

"Make new friends," my mother used to say when Mickey and Beth left our house together, cutting out the back door like a pair of dull knives. She refused to learn their names. She called them Becky and Mindy right to their faces. "Those two are morbid. What's the matter with them?" But I've never wanted other friends. I *like* what's wrong with the friends I have.

"You're beautiful now that you're thin," Beth said one afternoon before Christmas. Maybe she was drunk. We were sitting on the old vinyl couch, while, upstairs, my father could be heard in the kitchen, pacing, or marching in place. Mickey had poured a bit of filched gin into each of our diet Coke cans, and I was smoking without inhaling, just letting the smoke smear aimlessly across my mouth and face, roll off my tongue like a bitter cloud, or a big gray comma indicating a very long pause. The basement was cold, oozing with underground life, a clammy womb. There were only two windows in the finished section, and they let in just a little bit of cold prison light that, as soon as it crept in, was soaked up by the paneling and the gray carpet remnant.

"But you still act fat," Beth said.

I thought about that, looking down at my short corduroy skirt, black tights, soft white sweater. I knew I dressed, now, like a person who was thin. I looked good in the clothes I wore. I'd started to wear lipstick, shave my legs, blow my hair dry so that wisps of it flew around my face, flattering and framing it like the bright plastic face of a doll, but I still felt fat.

"It's my mother," I said. "She's inside me, with a balloon, waiting to blow me up." And I remembered going to the mall with her before Christmas one year when I was a child. She wanted me to sit in Santa's lap. I remembered how she handed me over to him, and how his arms felt warm, his lap was soft, and how the eyes lost in all that false beard were glassy, but very friendly. There were carols being sung somewhere above us, and the sound was fragile and full of light, like a glass straw held gently to a soprano's lips.

"Can I take this little girl home?" he asked my mother, and she snatched me back.

"He liked you because you're fat," my mother said.

"She liked me fat," I said.

"So did Phil," Beth said.

We are intimate. Beth and Mickey and I talk about only the most personal things—our periods, our parents, our dreams. By now, we've snooped into the darkest corners of each other's homes. Found each other's mother's diaphragms under the bathroom sink together—like flimsy

UFO's, or Playtex sand dollars, hinting vaguely of the sea, looking internal, but no more sexual than the plastic scrubbers with which those same mothers washed the dishes. And we were less impressed by the fact that our mothers might actually have sex with our fathers than by the possibility that something might still be generated from it. The possibility that fertility, for our mothers or for us, could go on for that long—little chickadees pecking nests in our uteruses forever.

We've seen each other's fathers in their underwear stumbling to the toilet late at night, half awake—gray specters of manliness in middle age, shameful and concave.

"I can't eat meatballs anymore," Mickey said one evening in the basement, "since I saw your father without his shorts on, Beth. Your father's balls look just like my mother's." And she waved her hand in the air as if to wave Mr. Warnke's awful balls away.

"You'll be sorry," my mother said. "These are the happiest days of your life, and you're not going to have anyone but those two Unsightlies to remember them by."

"I don't care," I said, and turned my back, as blank as a lost memory, to her.

And, I think, What does it matter that I'll never look back at my high school yearbook and recall, fondly, the dime-size faces of my classmates, the camaraderie of those days, the kegs thrown through plate-glass windows on Saturday nights when someone's trusting parents were out of town, or my name spray-painted red on the east wall of the high school, where those popular kids traditionally immortalize themselves and one another in big, goofy letters in the last months of their senior years: hearts and stars and exclamation points, until the janitor comes and whitewashes another year of popular kids off the cinder blocks with his bucket and brush?

It would be like being a rabbit, being one of those popular high school girls—trembling, ephemeral, just a vaporous urge full of hindsight, hopping. An essence, all bubble, whim, and vim slipped quickly in and out of a sock of bright, pretty fur, about to be ripped limb from limb by Time's stray dog.

Why even assume I'd *want* to be one of them?

Besides, my life in this place is swiftly ending. Already my college applications are in the mail. Four of them. Each with a carefully worded personal essay that begins, "I wish to attain the finest education I can, which, for me, means attending————."

In truth, college has always been the last place I wanted to go. It looms in my imagination as a kind of Emerald City full of sunglass-wearing rich kids with bandannas around their necks in the ice-green light of their Heineken bottles. At the center, an awful little man runs the show. Not a professor: an administrator, like my father. If you saw him, you would gasp in disappointment and sudden understanding.

Mickey and Beth can't wait to go. Phil doesn't plan to apply.

I HEAR MY FATHER PICK UP THE PHONE, WHICH HASN'T RUNG this early since the morning after my mother left, the morning she called to tell my father she was never coming back. I never actually heard it ring that time, and, I realize now, it's been months since the phone seemed like a likely way for my mother to contact us. I imagine, instead, skywriting, or telepathy, or a flock of birds in the bathtub as her method, at this point, of sending a message. I smudge the lid of my eye with mascara when I hear the phone ring, and have to wet a tissue to get it off.

Two years ago, when my father first filed the Missing Persons Report, the cops told us to stick close to the phone for a few weeks, told us we might get a call at any time, day or night, that it might be an emergency.

So, we got an answering machine, just in case we were out when the Big Call came, and my father recorded it with the only message we could think of, "No one's home right now. Please leave a message after the beep."

But no messages came from or about my mother, except the *shh-shh-shh* of no news.

The smudge on my eyelid looks like a bruise, and the harder I try to rub it off, the darker it gets, so I dot the other lid with mascara, too, and decide to make a determined action of it: black eye shadow. I hear my father say something into the phone downstairs in a throaty morning voice, and he hangs up quickly.

Later, in the car, headed toward the high school, my father identifies the mystery caller. He flexes and bends his gloved fingers around the steering wheel, staring straight ahead. January is turning to water all around us. When it freezes again, it will be dangerously slick. I remember seeing the parking lot of the Rite Aid rush into my face last year, and the sting of it on my palms. "The person who called," my father says, "was a woman."

There's a silence from him then that seems to suck the air in the car into it. I look at the side of his face. My father's hair is silver now—the color of dirty money. He's handsome. He does not look weak. When did he stop looking weak?

"Yeah?" I ask, and I know I sound surly. I'm a teenager. I'm not sure where my little-girl sweetness went. Like the weakness of my father, it simply vanished. I woke up one morning and it was gone.

He swallows. "Well. She is a textbook saleswoman I met at the office. She wants me to go to dinner with her."

I laugh out loud, then cover my mouth with my glove.

"Does that upset you?" my father asks, still looking fixedly into the firing squad in front of him.

"*Hell* no," I say. "Why shouldn't you go out with women, Dad? I'm thrilled you scored a date." I even touch his hand on the steering wheel: that's how much of an open-minded and supportive eighties kind of kid I am.

My father laughs a little to himself then, and it sounds like the laugh of a panicked man on a packed elevator, the needle dropping too fast, but not fast enough to scream yet: He still has to keep his cool.

"Good," he says, lightening up. He's wearing a tan coat over his blue suit and a red wool scarf around his neck.

"She's nice," he offers, tossing one hand in the air in my direction, as if throwing confetti, and I recognize my moment—this intimate space we're in and its potential for personal profit. Don't all teenage girls come equipped with radar for this?

"But, Dad," I say, "if I don't like her, do I get to give you as much shit about it as you give me about Phil?"

He checks the rearview mirror, puts the car into park in front of the high school, and sighs. Then he looks at me and says in a docile voice, thick with tongue, "I guess I should quit giving you what-for about Phil,"—making quotation marks in the air around "what-for"—"is that what you're saying?"

I raise my eyebrows and hum, "Mmm-hmm," and try to sparkle at him as I give him a quick kiss good-bye and bound out of the car.

I realize now that I'm playing the part of a vivacious daughter with a stern, worried, widowed father—although my quite-alive mother could very well be waiting for us right now back at the deserted ranch.

Would she care if, when she came back, my father had a girlfriend?

Was my mother a jealous wife?

Had she ever been? Had my mother ever had that feeling I used to have when I'd see Phil leaning up against his locker, some other girl—maybe Bonnie Pinter, who never wore a bra, whose lips were always wet and parted in a kind of permanent blow-job invitation—giggling into his face?

"You've got to be kidding," he'd say when I accused him of flirting with her. "She's a hose bag."

But I'd feel as if someone had stuffed my throat with cotton. I couldn't stand to think of him thinking of someone else. I could turn a corner in the hallway of that high school and see him standing in the glare, talking to Mickey, just Mickey, *my best friend*, and find myself riding that downward slope in my stomach, like a child on a tricycle, out of control, rolling down a hillside while something inaudible screamed inside me.

Had my mother ever felt like that?

When my father takes off his glove to wave good-bye, I see he's taken off his wedding ring. Just yesterday, at the dinner table, it was there.

I FEEL SURE THAT MY MOTHER WAS NEVER JEALOUS, SURE SHE did not think for one moment that another woman could take an interest in my father. To her, he must have seemed like the last man on the face of the earth any woman would want. Isn't it why she left in such a hurry, didn't even bother to take her purse?

Getting stuck with him wasn't even worth money, or credit cards, or lipsticks to her.

But *he* had been a jealous husband.

Once, at his golf league's end of summer picnic, my father drank three beers too fast before the hot dogs were done and, flushed, sweaty, longing to brag to his buddies about something—all of them richer men and better golfers—he'd blurted out, apropos of nothing, "My Evie hasn't gained a pound since we got married."

The other wives at this picnic gasped, feigning admiration, hyped-up envy, when all they really felt was dull loathing for my father, his boorish bragging, his drunken flush, and for his wife's slender body, sighing at her, "Oh, you make me sick," as if it were a compliment as their horny husbands looked her over slowly, and the hot dogs sizzled in their skins, and a mirage of fertilized heat hovered above the green. My father's cleats glinted in the sun, which set itself like a big red face in the west. Annoyed, my mother chewed a sour ice cube out of her vodka tonic and shot a look in my father's direction like a spray of silver thumbtacks in the air.

But what my father noticed was the looks the other men sent her, not the one she sent him. He wanted to brag, but he didn't want them to covet. He didn't understand why they would. Didn't they know she was his? He wasn't a religious man, but he knew all about *Thou shalt not stare at thy neighbor's wife*, and wouldn't do it. It wouldn't be polite.

And what were women to my father anyway? Hadn't he always been the kind of man who sees a rolling pasture, forty acres of wildflowers and red-winged blackbirds flitting from cattail to cattail in their brilliant epaulets, and thinks what a nice golf course it would make, where he would lay the sandtraps, what it would be like to ride those mowed, green hillocks in a cart?

So, on the drive home from the picnic, he sulked.

My mother looked out at the passing landscape, all blurred edges in the twilight and August fog, and refused to ask him what was wrong—a little woozy with vodka, waiting for him to talk the way you wait for the dentist to stuff a piece of cotton between your lip and gums.

"I don't like those guys looking at my wife," he finally blurted out.

"Well, maybe you shouldn't point me out, then, and encourage them to look," she said.

Silence.

He was thinking about golf courses—

Blackbirds and cattails and loosestrife once grew wild in the hills all over Ohio.

But what my father wanted was a smooth ride in a small motorized vehicle over domesticated pastures, plastic golf flags snapping in the breeze as they led you cheerfully from fairway to fairway, hole to hole.

THE GRANDMOTHERS MADE A BIG FUSS OVER MY FATHER AND me for Christmas. They stuffed our stockings with athletic socks. They made rice pudding. They played carols on the stereo all day, as if to drown out the white noise of a winter afternoon with shouting.

"*HARK the herald angels sing . . .* "

All day, a standing rib roast hissed and spit in the oven. The smell of scorched flesh, the domestic torture of a burning cow made our mouths water for hours before we ate it.

Phil came over with Mrs. Hillman just before the grandmothers piled the table with meat and relishes and pudding and bread, and they pretended that Mrs. Hillman was not blind, and that my father did not treat Phil like a mortal enemy—staring when Phil wasn't looking, then looking away when Phil looked back.

"Merry, *merry* Christmas," Marilyn said, raising a crystal glass of champagne above her head. We raised our glasses, too—my parents' wedding crystal—and they caught the light from the ceiling and flashed it around the table as small, sharp pieces of air and water in our faces. When a bit of champagne spilled over the rim of Mrs. Hillman's glass into my father's mashed potatoes, Phil rolled his eyes.

"Brock, you eat some more roast," Marilyn said to my father, her son. But, next to me, my father looked pale before the mounds of food, which were hidden under pot lids and plastic wrap. He looked like a man at a feast for the dead—afraid of the food, surrounded by the ghosts of Christmas past: hazy females shaking fists at him, or a host of Virgin Marys in their blue robes, tapping their toes impatiently, visibly annoyed to be waiting in a manger, somewhere else to go.

There's always been a bit of the scrooge in my father anyway—the miser, the worrier. He's always been the kind of man who'd try to haggle the price of a Christmas tree down from twenty dollars to ten, standing outside the trailer that was set up in the supermarket parking lot, puffing at the tree salesman, who was unshaven in a flannel work shirt, shaking his head *no, no, no* in the piney cold, the smell of sap, as my mother and I waited for my father back in the car, windows rolled up, heat blower stuffing our throats with dried-up air.

My father would come back to the car red-faced, without a tree, and say, "Let's go somewhere else." My mother would look down at her leather gloves then, the muscle in her jaw pulsing.

"But, Daddy," I might have said, "that one was *perfect.*"

And it had been: full-branched, smelling green and genial.

It didn't matter.

We'd come home with a ten-dollar tree. The sickly twin of the one my father refused to buy.

Of course, someone being generous might have called my father *practical.* After all, we weren't rich, really. He made a fine salary, but my mother didn't work. And the mortgage on our house in Garden Heights was no small price to pay for a quiet suburb and a big garage. We paid a price to be surrounded by quiet, as if it were a jagged wall of diamonds.

So, someone generous might have pointed out that my father was looking out for us—socking it away for my college education, making sure we had nice clothes and sturdy furniture. He was a man who knew what waste was—how it accumulated in the emptiness you made for it: heaps of gnawed bones, empty tin cans, used paper plates, overpriced trees you only kept around for two weeks before hauling them to the dump—and he hated waste.

But my mother never saw him, never described him, in a flattering light. She used to call my father her wet blanket—

"*How* much did the new curtains cost?" my father would ask, standing open-mouthed before them after she'd spent the whole day hanging blinds, ruffles, rods.

As he left the room, she'd watch his back. "My wet blanket," she'd say, and I pictured my father flattened by a steamroller, like a cartoon character—a drenched square of pale flesh with just his face still sticking up.

My father the bearskin rug.

———————

At the dinner table this year, my father wore his familiar Christmas grimace, as if the expense of it had whittled his teeth down to painful nubs.

He'd given his mother and mother-in-law matching clock radios, and I'd gotten one, too, along with a little change purse with some cash crammed into it. "Buy yourself something you want," he said while the tree blinked in his eyes. I didn't count the bills.

"Have more, more," one of the grandmothers said, pushing the roast toward him.

My father fished around the platter of beef with a fork, but took only one gray knuckle of hard fat, and then he cut it into two gelatinous halves, which he put in his mouth, sucking on each one for a while before he swallowed.

"So," MICKEY SAYS, "IF YOU FIND THE DETECTIVE THAT attractive, why don't you go to his office and seduce him?"

We're smoking menthol cigarettes in my mother's station wagon in the high school parking lot. A minty scarf of smoke floats above us like something my mother might have worn home from her dentist's office on a spring day.

"You've got to be kidding," I say. "He's at least forty years old. Even if I *could* seduce him, couldn't he go to jail for making it with a high school girl?"

"No," Mickey says, considering this seriously. She looks like an accountant going over some numbers in the distance of the windshield. She's wearing her cheerleading outfit, and her legs are bare and mottled with cold under the green-and-gold pleated skirt. Her short white socks are regulation, just above the ankle, and her leather coat is zipped up over a big green *R*. It's basketball season again, those long months of muggy gyms, the smell of sweaty jockstraps, the rumbling thunder of bleachers and screaming muffled by cinder blocks.

Because Mickey is a cheerleader, if I wanted to swim across the Atlantic Ocean, she'd urge me on, she'd convince me I could do it without a problem: Am I seriously considering her advice?

She advises, "I don't think so. I think the age of consent in Ohio is sixteen. Besides, Kat, he's a fucking *detective*. Surely he could figure out some way to avoid getting *caught*."

"What about Phil?" I ask her.

"What *about* Phil?" she asks me back, and we both start to laugh.

Laughing, she says, "Give Phil the old heave-ho, like the one your mother gave your father."

I stop laughing. I think about my mother.

"Kat," Mickey says. "I'm sorry. Shouldn't I have said that?"

"Where *do* you think your mother is?" Zeena asked me as we cleared the Christmas feast from the table and slipped the greasy dishes into gray sink water.

"Grandma," I said, sounding impatient, "I have no idea."

"Your father looks awful," she said, licking a little gravy from the ladle before rinsing it off. "I left two husbands, God knows, but never like this. I told them where I was going."

Marilyn appeared behind us then. She said, "But that

wouldn't be Evie's style." She shook her head sadly. "Evie would want to just disappear, to just *poof*"—and she made a starburst with her fingers, as if she were sprinkling the air with magic dust—"be gone."

Zeena took a dishcloth out of a drawer, and smelled it, then looked at me. She said, "Wager a guess, Kat," holding the checkered rag in one hand, wagging it cheerfully, "about your mother. Just a guess—where could she be?"

Always the gambler, Zeena.

Okay, I thought. Okay. Why not?

Wager a guess—

I was game to try.

I narrowed my eyes and thought hard for a while as my grandmothers looked at me, but the only thing that came to mind was the message on a billboard we used to pass on the highway on the way to the mall. It said, in stern black letters, THE WAGES OF SIN IS DEATH.

I just shook my head. I said, "Sorry, Grandma, I can't even guess."

"Fair enough," she said.

The next day, their planes left for opposite ends of the country at the exact same time, the grandmothers 40,000 feet above the earth in identical tin cans with wings, unzipping the clouds and the precipitation and the gray Midwestern sky between them.

Phil and I drove them to the airport through a miniature blizzard on a Tuesday afternoon. He and I sat in front, Phil driving, while the grandmothers held each other's hands in the backseat. Zeena was wearing a denim dress and boots. Marilyn had her rabbit jacket zipped up, hood over her red hair, and, in it, she looked like a pet, which, when you brought it home from the pet store, you hadn't expected to grow. You'd gone and bought something small and cuddly for your kid, but it kept getting bigger. And wilder. Maybe even a little mean. The highway scrolled its sooty cold ahead of us.

"Maybe your flights will be canceled," I said over my shoulder, "because of the weather."

"No way," Zeena said, and Marilyn also shook her head. "No flight I've ever been booked on has ever been canceled."

"Me either," said Marilyn.

In the backseat of Phil's father's car, the grandmothers looked radiant, as if old age had embraced them with light, like two filaments in two lightbulbs—that kind of bright incarceration, each one in her loose cage of glass.

Where *was* my mother? I wondered.

I tried to think. But the possibilities seemed as uncountable as the stars, and to try to consider them all at once was like trying to decide where the universe might end or who invented God if God invented the world, like trying to see something white on white.

"What *is* infinity?" Mrs. Valentine asked us one day in Geometry as she drew a perfect chalk circle on the blackboard with a compass. No one raised a hand. And when I tried to think of an answer in the silence of that classroom, I found myself suspended and dizzy above my own brain, which did not seem to be contained by my skull any longer, but which drifted above me, invisible and *uncontainable*, without questions, let alone answers, only hinting at its possibilities through dreams and half glimpses of things I thought, briefly, I might have seen.

These thoughts of infinity exhausted me, as it did to look up at that perfectly empty circle on the blackboard, Mrs. Valentine waiting for an answer as I considered where my mother might be.

That circle was like the *O* on the cover of my mother's book, *Achieving Orgasm.*

Or the *O* in Ohio—the big one, separated forever from the small one by a perfunctory salutation. *Hi.*
Hello.

As I stared into that circle, singular flakes of snow seemed to blow through my imagination, tossed around in the wind of it, some of it settling, some of it lifting and falling like a veil in front of my face, or a ribbon of breath I was chasing—trying to catch it, trying to keep it, in a flimsy Dixie cup.

"WHAT DO *YOU* THINK?" DR. PHALER ASKS. "DO *YOU* THINK your mother might have been having an affair?"

"I don't know," I say. "I don't know what I think about my mother."

But what I think is this:

She was a housewife, *his* housewife.

For twenty years she served his dinner at six o'clock. Afterward, she washed the dinner dishes in Palmolive, to keep her hands soft. One Christmas when he offered to buy her a dishwasher she insisted she would never use it, that washing her husband's dinner dishes by hand was one of the greatest pleasures a woman could have. And he had no idea she was being sarcastic.

This is what I know about my father:

When they were first engaged, he would have wanted his mother and brothers to see her dressed up and wearing his ring—an unimaginative diamond solitaire, quarter carat, the kind of engagement ring jewelers keep in a velvet-lined drawer labeled *Tightwads*. He liked the way it looked on her finger. A bit of smudged light he'd given her for agreeing to be his wife.

Simple, it made a simple statement about him on her hand.

Sometimes, he'd write my mother's new name under his on a scrap of paper:

Brock Connors
Evie Connors

Then, *Mr. and Mrs. Brock Connors.*

Then, the one that hurt her teeth to see, *Mrs. Brock Connors*—as if, by marrying, my father would be himself, and also become her.

Newly engaged, waiting for the Big Day the way you wait for a pleasant dentist jangling his tray of silver instruments your way—all that necessary pain—perhaps my mother imagined herself in a white apron in the suburbs, wearing a pleated poodle skirt, hair pulled back in a glistening bun, plugging a vacuum cleaner in and being sucked up.

"So, why did she marry him?" Dr. Phaler asks.

"Because," I say, "he was there. And he wanted to marry her."

She was twenty-seven, a receptionist at Waterhouse Steel, and lived with her father, who built model airplanes in his study all day. At night, he would fly a radio-controlled helicopter around the house—sweating as he did, manning the operations nervously, knocking over lamps, breaking things.

When she was hired at Waterhouse Steel, the company president assured her she'd have a long and promising future there, but five years later she still spent every day at the reception desk, answering the phone, listening to the other secretaries behind her whisper about layoffs and pay cuts, voices full of asthma and nervous itching.

"Waterhouse Steel. How may I direct your call?" she asked hundreds of times a day.

She even said it in her sleep. But in her dreams, there was no one on the other end of the line when she answered, just the sound of blood pumping in her own ear. Her own blood. Pale and pumping. A little wind, too. A bit of static—as if, far away, a small brown bird with dry and wiry feet was hopping across a waxy sheet of sandwich wrap on its way to her.

And she began to think the sound of that emptiness might be the music of her future—

Weather, nasty birds, and nothing.

She'd gone to college, and she'd done well. She'd received some modest attention. For English 472, her senior year, she wrote a paper about Blake's *Songs of Innocence and Songs of Experience* entitled "Sacrificial Lamb," which was prefaced by a quote from "The Tyger":

Did he who made the Lamb make thee?

The paper considered the dual nature of human existence as it was depicted in the songs. And Professor Norman Owen, who was a minor poet in his spare time— gray-bearded but with a rippling chest of muscles he must have spent a fair portion of his working life developing— read my mother's paper out loud on the last day of class and even asked her to stand afterward as her classmates clapped. Through most of the semester she'd sat in the back, taking notes, and he hadn't spoken a word to her, nor had he any reason to until that day.

"Eve," he said, handing the paper back to her, "splendid work!"

It was what he'd written on the bottom of it, too:

Eve, Splendid work! A +

And that was that.

After class, he left the auditorium where he lectured, dogged by three or four young men—all of them bespectacled, white shirts tucked sloppily into their pencil-legged pants, huffing seriously about "The Waste Land" all the way back to Professor Owen's office with him.

This was 1962.

The next day, her father came to pick her up in Columbus, happy to see her, happy to be carrying her clothes and books in flimsy cardboard boxes out of her little dorm room with its peeling walls, bringing her home with her A+ paper and a degree on a piece of parchment that smelled like stale cake.

When they got back to their old farmhouse outside Toledo, when they'd hauled her things back to her childhood bedroom, my mother's father collapsed on their sagging couch and said, "Thank God that's over!"

Meaning college.

How had it come and gone so fast?

She'd barely blinked, and she was back.

So, my mother'd had an education. She'd wandered through one of the largest libraries in Ohio for four years: all those yellow pages eaten up by worms and doubts, and that musty air in her hair when she went back to the dorm to sleep.

She'd never gotten into a sorority. For four years she'd studied English and worked in a cafeteria, cutting squares of Jell-O and spice cake with a flat knife, then placing them carefully under the chilled cafeteria glass.

Why the idea of a real career never came to her in those years between college and my father, I do not know.

Why she didn't do something later with her good education is a puzzle. It must have been a puzzle even to her. Those four years in college, perhaps they turned, after five years at Waterhouse Steel, into a cool and trembling cube in her mind. Perhaps she was afraid, after all that time, to turn it over in her memory, afraid to lay it out again on the plain, white, cafeteria plate of her life.

Her job was dull.

Her father was not a talker.

She'd started to look for excitement in Toledo bars at night, looking for a man, looking for a future. She was beautiful, and smart. A sexy, witty, desperate woman.

Once, in a magazine I picked up in a dentist's waiting room—perhaps Dr. Heine's office, waiting for my mother, perhaps *Woman's Day*—I read a statistic that surprised me: The most likely place for an American woman in her mid-twenties to die is in the passenger seat of a car.

I tried to imagine it. All across America, young women in passenger seats, watching the continent roll past them from those car windows, counting crows, and cows, and rest stops, crossing and uncrossing their legs, flipping the mirrored sun visor down to get a look at themselves— pretty, lipsticked, hair tucked neatly behind their ears— while some man drives them somewhere they may or may not want to go. To a bar, to a movie, to bed.

For a while, my mother was one of them.

She was single, twenty-seven, a receptionist at Waterhouse Steel. She lived in a farmhouse on the outskirts of Toledo with her father, who was turning into an old man. She needed to get married, but what she wanted was excitement, and there she was, trying to find it, night after night in the passenger seat of some bass player's, or pilot's, or Marine on leave's car.

I could easily imagine my mother as a young woman in the passenger seat of that car. There it was. All that trust in nothing, like faith in God, letting this guy decide when to change lanes, letting this guy (and maybe he's been drinking beer all night, maybe he's stoned out of his mind—which, even sober, was never razor sharp) roll through the intersection under a blinking light.

Like faith in God—only he's no god. He's wearing plaid pants. He flunked out of high school, or he studied marketing in college. Maybe he fails to see the semi, bearing down, or he flips the car he's driving, with that young woman beside him, into a ditch. Perhaps, before they come to rescue her with the Jaws of Life (she's pinned in the wreckage while he smokes a cigarette at the side of the road, feeling bad about what happened, telling the cops it was an accident) she sees it all flash before her eyes. She thinks, *This was bound to happen.* There's blood, and something worse—something soft and squidlike—on her tongue, and then it's done.

"Is this Eve?" my father asked when he called one week after they'd met in the lounge of the Franklin Hotel. He'd been there for a conference. She'd been there to watch a bass player she'd been dating.

"Do you like to dance?" she asked him on their first date. They sat in the red vinyl booth of a restaurant downtown. My father chased a rack of ribs, bloody with barbecue sauce, around on his plate with a knife. His hands were slick.

"No," he said, shaking his head.

My mother pushed her plate away and put her hands in her lap. She imagined herself with a diamond on her hand saying, "I quit," to the president of Waterhouse Steel. But she couldn't look across the table at my father, who had a red gash of sauce stretching from the corner of his mouth to his ear.

"I'm sorry," Dr. Phaler says, "our time is up."

I'M WEARING A NIGHTGOWN MADE OF FOG, AND I'M INVISIBLE in it. My mother dusts my bedroom with a huge fan of feathers, and the motion, the wind she's lifting, billows around me.

"Mom," I say, "stop. I'm going to blow away."

But she doesn't hear or see me.

She's dusting the top of my dresser, and the windowsills, and the corners of the floor. A cyclone of dust is kicked up by her feathers, and somehow I know that, really, it's my father she's trying to dust out. I can tell by the angry trembling of those feathers, the way she shakes them like a soft fist all around her all at once, making a storm of the calm. But I'm only fog—

I feel my feet lift off the ground.

She opens the window, and I feel myself sifted into a million little wisps, drifting out the screen.

Slipping past her I say, "I was there, too, but you didn't see me."

"I KNOW SHE DIDN'T HAVE ORGASMS," I TELL DR. PHALER.

Though there is only the slightest change in her professional expression (What is it? A minute widening of the eyes? A barely registered raising of the eyebrows?) I can see she's interested. "How do you know?" she asks in a tone of total composure, as if her voice is coated with wax.

"There's a book, in her dresser, in a shoe box, *Achieving Orgasm: A Woman's Guide.*"

"What made you look in her dresser?"

"Oh." I shrug. "I looked in it years ago. I was curious."

"Have you looked there since? Is the book still there?"

"Yes," I say.

"Do you think there's something significant about this?"

"I'm not sure," I say. "I guess it's just more evidence of her dissatisfaction. Her frustration, I guess. I guess her sex life with my father must have been pretty dull."

"What does this mean to *you*?"

I think for a long time. I think of my mother reading that book in the afternoon while my father was at work, while I was at school. She spilled coffee on it, broke the spine, then shoved it back in her drawer, in that shoe box, to hide it—but she couldn't have learned anything she didn't already know:

You need to relax, it urged.

You need to learn to let go.

You need to believe you deserve pleasure, then go off in search of it.

The book was full of silly, New Age suggestions:

When no one is at home, take a long, naked look at yourself in a full-length mirror, and tell yourself you love what you see. Say it out loud. Say, "I love my body," to yourself. Say, "I love you,———," to your mirror.

I couldn't imagine my mother doing that. I couldn't *stand* to imagine my mother doing that.

"She was getting older," I say to Dr. Phaler, but my voice sounds far away. "She didn't want to die like that."

"Like what?" Dr. Phaler asks. I see her through a scrim of cold ash, as if we are in one of those plastic globes of snow, shaken.

"She was tired of baking Christmas cookies"—and, up on Dr. Phaler's ceiling tiles, I see all those sheets and tins and ovens full of cookies, all that frozen dough in the freezer. I remember Hansel and Gretel's witch in the woods. How her house was made of candy and cake, and how she was crippled with rage.

And I remember how, when Phil and I had been dating for only a few months, my mother came downstairs one night while we were making out on the couch.

Back then, our bodies were like two plants growing everywhere at once, getting closer and closer, twining and choking and groping—writhing in the night, unfurling enormous leaves in the dark, thorns and flowers and birds' nests—swiftly, but in slow motion. I suppose she could smell us from her bed above us, the panting and rustling, the sound of pores expanding, oozing hormones, drooling into each other's hair.

When we noticed she was standing on the stairs, looking down on us, we panicked, and sat up fast. I pulled my sweater back down around me. Phil zipped up his pants. But my lips were engorged, obscene, a sexual organ.

"Mom," I said.

"Yes," she said. *"C'est moi."*

She wasn't wearing a robe, just a nightgown, and she came downstairs slowly and stood before us. The only light that was on was behind her, and her body was outlined— a solid, dark silhouette of hips and breasts—under the thin silk. I noticed Phil look up, then look away, too fast.

"Listen," she said. "Do what you have to do down here, kids, but don't spot my couch, okay?"

I looked down.

Phil flinched.

Maybe, back in bed above us, she lay awake and listened to the dark.

The whole house was breathing hard. The furnace, snoring dust. That freezer in the basement—like agitation, frozen stiff. Water slowly rising in the toilet tank. The humming of the fuse box. The tight, silent whine of the telephone line stretching into the night.

My father slept restlessly beside her, and she could hear his toes rustle under the covers.

She hated those toes.

Then, the darkness under her seemed to expand:

She could tell we were at it again. Clawing, clutching—

Maybe she remembered seeing Phil that first time, the day she went to introduce herself to his mother. How he'd descended the stairs shirtless, just a feather ridge of hair along his breastbone. Naturally muscled. The muscles of a boy, not a bodybuilder. Maybe she saw herself wearing a long-lost and forgotten dress—gauzy, embroidered with pale glue pearls. *Now where did I wear that?* she thought, and then it all came back: the Kleenex and lotion in her purse, the sentimental music, some boy's big hands moving over her like the flu. She had been sick with kisses.

And the darkness below her seemed to rise like dough—flour and yeast and water mixed up with night.

We were down there in that darkness, that darkness that might rise and rise, and push everything out of its way as it rose, as it pushed its way out of the living room, swelling up the stairs. It might smother her in her sleep with its sprawling, domestic flesh. Maybe she was thinking about that, and couldn't possibly sleep with us below her, doing that.

When we heard her descending the stairs again, we pulled our clothes together, and Phil fled.

"Go to bed," she hissed at me between her teeth as I passed her on the stairs.

"It's why she left," I say to Dr. Phaler just as my time runs out.

"I BOUGHT A BIRD," MY MOTHER TOLD MY FATHER WHEN she got home one Saturday from the mall. "It's in the car."

"What?" he asked, then asked again, "What?"

"I said," she said, pronouncing each world carefully, "I bought a bird."

Phil and I came down the stairs then. Perhaps we looked tousled, mutually pawed. At that point, my father was still naive, and he let us stay up there all day with the door closed. He must have thought we were playing an intensive game of chess, one that left us sweaty and short of breath.

"Go get it for me, would you?" my mother said to Phil, who was used to taking orders from women. His blind mother issued them from her armchair all day, and that was why he spent so much time at our house—nosing through our kitchen for cheese and cold meat.

And every night, he stayed for dinner, and liked to eat—complimenting my mother's cooking with every bite he took, *mmm*-ing and nodding. She liked that, and started making dishes she'd never made for my father and me— mignon Alfonse, beef medallions l'orange, chicken in wine, letting the chicken stew a long time in a whole bottle of burgundy until the soaked meat shed like wet feathers from the bones—slippery, tinged with purple—and the kitchen smelled like a shelter for drunks, humid with booze, warm and debauched.

Phil's mother was a terrible cook—couldn't measure, couldn't see the color or the texture of the food she made, so that, even with Phil's help in the kitchen, her tuna cas- serole might turn out as green and soupy as a meal made of swamp, her chicken breasts burnt black in a pan—and Phil ate everything my mother made as if he'd never eaten.

My father, of course, couldn't tell Hamburger Helper from mignon Alfonse, and I had gotten so used to dieting, back when I was fat, that what I saw when I looked at a plate of food was a graph of calories, a calculation of ounces and grams, how many laps around the neighborhood such a meal would cost.

We were never the eaters she wanted us to be. Too stupid, too selfish, or too afraid. So my mother finally had in Phil the audience she'd always wanted. At these last suppers, which were clearly prepared in Phil's honor, my father would look down at his plate, confused, fork poised over an inebriated wing, as if he'd just been deported to a foreign country. But Phil would shovel it in, leaning over intently, as if he were washing his face in my mother's meal.

Once, my mother told me to invite Phil's mother over, too. But when I did, Mrs. Hillman just shook her head and made the corners of her mouth into little, irritable pyramids. "No," she said, "I don't like your mother."

"The bird's in a cage in the backseat," my mother said to Phil. "Be careful carrying it in."

Phil shrugged and said, "Sure."

He was wearing a plaid flannel shirt and jeans. His hair was bright, and little slivers of blond shimmered on his chin and upper lip. He hadn't shaved for a day or two.

"What kind of bird?" I asked.

She said, "You'll see."

The bird was a canary. Simple and white. It had quivered in my mother's palm at the pet store in the mall like a mouse, like a milkweed pod splitting with silk, or a feathered change purse full of blood and hollow bones. Its eyes were black beads, and they darted around the pet store while that bird sat scratch-scratching its wire feet in my mother's hand, scanning the place for cats, or planning its escape, thinking, *Now's my big chance.*

But it couldn't fly away. The pet store girl had shown my mother how to hold it. "Here," she said, "like this," placing my mother's palm over its wings, "so you can't cut off his breath."

The girl was young, wearing a tight dress. Her hair was black, and she had a little, clipped nose.

My mother held the bird the way the pet store girl had shown her, and she could feel its heart against her lifeline, quivering like a little finger in its sleek chest. She popped it back into the cage and said to the pet store girl, "I'll take it."

That canary snapped its head mechanically, like a wind-up toy, taking this new information in.

"And a cage?" the girl asked. "Do you have a cage?"

"No. I need a cage, and food, a bird-care book, all that."

My mother took her credit card out of her purse, and the girl started pulling things off the shelves for her. Rape seed. Millet. Bath dish. Perching stick. It made my mother happy. She gave the girl her credit card with a smile as she rang up the purchases. And as the bird chirped nervously near the cash register in its cage, my mother wandered into the back of the store and watched an aquarium full of small silver fish dart in and out of the ceramic mouth of a shark. She'd let the girl pick out the cage, and it was the most expensive one—the size and shape of a hatbox, a high one, a hatbox made for a hat with feathers and fruit and lilacs on top.

"This is your guarantee that," the girl said, showing my mother a piece of paper, "the bird is a male. If it doesn't sing within fourteen days, you can bring it back for an exchange. But," she said, "if you think you'll want to do that, we have to mark the bird, so we know it's the same bird you bought."

My mother considered it for a moment—the guarantee, the marking.

"No," she said, looking at her new bird's pure white wing. It had its head tucked under there. She didn't know how they marked birds, and didn't ask. "I won't be bringing it back."

The girl threw the guarantee with its gold seal away, and said, "Enjoy your canary, ma'am."

My mother carried the canary out of the mall like a lantern held in front of her. A hurricane lamp. Perhaps she looked like a Victorian ghost come back to haunt the mall in her wool coat, a thin and mysterious smile on her lips, headed somewhere with her bright urge in a cage. Children stumbled at the ends of their parents' arms, pointing at the bird, wanting her to stop, but she kept walking.

It was only early November, but Muzak Christmas carols were piping down from the ceiling—high up, near the fluorescent lights—saccharine, slippery, frivolous, sounding lubricated and faraway, as if a choir of angels had been shipped to Ohio from heaven in aluminum cans: exhausted containers of angels, like poultry, chicken feathered, passionless, disoriented. They'd been brought here against their wills, forced to spend their days warbling about God from some crawl space above the mall—

With feeling, my mother imagined the maestro of Corporate Christmas Carols screaming, stomping his foot, waving his baton madly over them in the air.

But that languid music, that spiritless serenade, oozed from the ceiling.

And when she left the mall for the parking lot, my mother passed Santa near the entrance. He was smoking a cigarette. His eyes were big, as if he were medicated, or insane. "Good-looking bird," he said, and wiped his nose on the back of his black glove.

She'd bought a miniskirt, too, before the bird—suede, taupe. It was in a bag with the bird book and bird food, slung over her other arm. She hadn't even tried it on. She'd just seen it waiting there, and bought it. She pictured herself wearing it, sitting in that fat man's lap.

She was happy.

She hadn't had a pet since I'd grown up.

After Phil brought it in, my mother set the bird up handsomely, royally, next to my father's La-Z-Boy in the den—its little water dish, its lettuce bowl, its perching stick. All day that canary kept its head tucked under its wing. It didn't sing, but my mother was perfectly willing to wait those fourteen days. She was in no hurry to hear it sing. She had waited longer for more important things.

"YOU LIKE?" SHE ASKED, PRESENTING HER MINISKIRT TO THE den. It was a Sunday. My father and Phil were watching football. I was doodling into a math book with a pencil, legs tucked up under me on the couch. I'd thrown a piece of pale lettuce fringe to the canary, who pecked apathetically at it. That canary had no appetite at all.

She was wearing sheer black panty hose. Black heels. A black turtleneck. And that miniskirt.

"Well?" she said.

My father looked up from the football game like a man who'd been slapped on the ass with a towel. Phil looked sheepishly at my mother's shoes. I was stunned, looking from her good legs up to her bright face. She was flushed. Her hair was all done up, and she had a dark smear of lipstick on her lips. On the television there was a close-up of a girl with a shredded burst of pom-pom in her fist. Cheering. She must have been shaking it into the camer-aman's face.

"Pretty sexy for forty-six, don't you think?" my mother asked.

I crossed my arms and looked away.

My father's mouth was open.

Phil was nodding yes.

"HAVE A SEAT," DETECTIVE SCIEZIESCIEZ SAYS, HANGING MY coat on a hook near his door, which he's already shut. He's wearing a starched white shirt, maroon tie, loosened, and his sleeves are rolled up. His forearms are thick. He has a tattoo on the left one, "USMC."

The detective's office is warm, and smells like leather, musky. The office of a man. His desk is cluttered with papers, piles of envelopes torn open, pens, street maps, and a metal box of Band-Aids. He's wearing a Band-Aid across the knuckles of his right hand. His oak desk chair rocks as he leans backward, and I sit across from him in a plastic chair.

It's six o'clock in the evening, and I can see the sky behind him through a window, which is open just a crack. That sky is spatulate and turning blue-black but sparked with small, hard, flakes of snow. We are on the seventeenth floor of his office building in downtown Toledo, and I think I can actually hear the place where the wind starts. We are that close.

Detective Scieziesciez takes out a notepad and a pen,

leans forward on his desk, and writes something at the top of a page. The Band-Aid on his knuckles ripples as he writes. "I'm so glad you got in touch and could come down here," he says. "You don't mind if I take notes while we talk?"

"No," I say, and look down at the buttons on my blouse. They are flat and gold, and I can see my face reflected in them. Seven buttons, seven faces. I am wearing the taupe miniskirt my mother bought when she bought her canary.

"Okay," he says happily, leaning forward, looking at me. "Where should we start?"

"Well," I say, trying to sound serious, and intelligent, and worried, but my voice sounds weightless to me. I feel so far up in the sky. As I rode the elevator here, I felt light-headed, and tired, as if I were flying for the first time. Now, my voice sounds like tissue caught in my mouth. "I called because I thought maybe I had some information. About my mother."

"Of course." He nods professionally. His jaw is dark with the stubble of the beard he must have shaved this morning, growing back already, just like the first time I saw him. A strong jaw. His eyes are also dark, and his eyebrows are raised. I can smell him. Salt and sweat and deodorant soap. And it makes my heart pump as hard as a shark swimming fast in my blood.

I watch the detective's pen move over his pad of paper as I speak. I say, "I've been thinking. I've been thinking my mother might have been having an affair when she left. I've remembered some things."

The detective writes this down. I look at his arms. From the elbows down, they are bare, resting on his desk. He looks up at me, pleased, and says, "Tell me more, sweetheart."

"I DON'T LIKE THAT CANARY," MY FATHER SAID. IT WAS perched on my mother's little finger, feet curled up tightly, and it made nervous pecking motions in my father's direction, as if it were sewing something invisible between them in the air.

"You don't like that canary," my mother sang to the tune of "Jimmy Crack Corn," "and I don't care."

"What's wrong with you?" he asked, seeming sincerely perplexed.

The canary shivered in her hand, as if a smaller, colder bird had darted across its grave. It looked frail, and my mother laughed out loud at my father in a sudden, cackling snicker.

"And what were you doing wearing that miniskirt?" he asked.

"You didn't like it?" The canary crept up her blouse, making its way to her dark hair, tiny eye traveling over her enormous blue eye, taking it in, trying to imagine exactly what my mother was:

Not a bird.

Not a plane.

"Get that thing out of here," my father said, grabbing at it.

The bird began to flap its white wings.

"Get your goddamn paws off my canary," she said, slapping his hands away. "I'll wear whatever the hell I want."

On my father's face, there was a puzzled expression, cheeks pulled in, a puffy pucker, as if he'd eaten a spoonful of something, and now it was moving around, still alive, in his mouth.

"ARE YOU FUCKING HIM?" SHE ASKED, STANDING IN THE doorway. I was on my back in bed, under the covers, in the dark.

"Jesus Christ," I hissed in a low whisper, and rolled onto my side, turning my back to her. "Get out of here."

"No," she said, stepping into my bedroom and shutting the door behind her. It became pitch black in the room. I closed my eyes. From all the way in the basement, I could hear that canary screeching. Two days earlier, it had learned to warble, then the warbling had turned to horrible shrieking all day and night. We'd put the bird's cage in the basement to escape it. "Well?" she said. "Is Phil good in bed?"

I said nothing, pulled the covers a little higher. I was naked and cool in my sheets. As a baby, I'd worn zip-up sleepers with feet. As a little girl, she'd dressed me in Victorian nightgowns. Now, whatever I was wearing when I got in bed, I took it off and threw it on the floor. I liked the feeling of nothing but my skin between the sheets and me.

"Well?" she said again. "Is Phil a good fuck?"

"What do you know about fucking?" I said. I could hear her inhale when I said it, as if the words had shocked her, though to me they'd sounded flat, rehearsed, as if I'd read them from a piece of paper someone offstage had just handed me. I didn't even really know what I meant. For a split second I'd considered saying something about that book in her drawer, the one about achieving orgasms, but I had no idea what to say.

Suddenly, my mother flipped the light switch, and the whole room was exposed. She came to the edge of my bed, yanking the sheets and blankets off. I rolled onto my back, and grabbed them, struggling to pull them up again, but she kept them in her fists.

"What *is* this?" My mother was screaming. "What *is* this?" She tore the covers off completely, and they fell at the foot of my bed in a pile. "Why aren't you dressed?"

I put my arms across my breasts, sat up, pulled my legs up to my chest, scrambling away from her. Her face was as white as a window shade. My heart was beating hard, and I was crying, shaking. "I was hot." I said. "What do you care? What difference does it make?"

"It makes a difference to me that my daughter has become a slut." She spat at me. Hands scratching in my direction, but missing me.

I was gasping. I couldn't catch my breath.

"Mom." I sobbed it. "Stop it. Stop."

But she pummeled my shoulders with her fists— softly. Her fists felt soft. I tried to grab her wrists. Finally, she stopped, but she was panting hard with a dry and hollow sound.

"I know about fucking," she said—faraway, defeated— before she backed away from my bed.

"What is the matter with you?" I screamed at her back as she left.

WE ATE IN HUMMING SILENCE. MY FATHER MASTICATING, Phil nodding and *mmm*-ing at my mother as I slid a piece of parsley around and around on my plate.

She'd made crabmeat thermidor over toasted Holland rusk, and the garnish of blanched almonds looked like fingernails burnt to a crisp.

Afterward, I went upstairs to change clothes. Phil and I were going to a movie. My father was on the toilet—his first stop every night right after he ate. He'd get up from the dining room table, say, "Excuse me," and go directly to the bathroom to eliminate: The king upon his throne, my mother called it.

Phil was helping her clear the table.

He'd taken his sweatshirt off for dinner, as if dinner were a relay race or a basketball scrimmage, as if there were a trophy to win, and eating so much so fast made him sweat. The T-shirt he wore was tight, and his muscles were under it, right there, impossible not to notice. There was blond hair on his arms. You could even see his stomach muscles, how they rode all the way down into his pants.

My mother was wearing jeans, a wine-red sweater, and lipstick to match. She could hear water rush in the toilet, dragging my father's waste away.

He was pulling up his pants, all done.

She could hear me bump around upstairs.

Phil had a stack of plates and greasy knives.

She blocked his path in the doorway between the dining room and the kitchen, and said, "Either I made too much, or you didn't eat enough."

He laughed, but he was nervous.

"Half of this is going to end up in Tupperware," she said, taking the plate of crabmeat thermidor out of his hands.

When I came downstairs, they looked at me. I saw a napkin in my mother's hand with her lipstick on it. My mother's smile smeared off and crumpled up.

A ruined fist of it between them. Phil cleared his throat.

"What are you staring at?" she asked.

Many years before, my mother had been invited to a neighborhood Tupperware party, where she'd bought a whole set of it. The hostess of the party was the wife of one of my father's golf buddies—a jowly, middle-aged man with the high shine of an alcoholic: rosy nose, buffed cheeks. He was away on business when his wife invited the other wives over to buy stackable plastic, but the smell of the man was all over the house—Listerine and whiskey and cigars. The hostess greeted her guests at the door of her Garden Heights home wearing a black dress and pearls— though she looked exhausted, worried. Her face was as unlined as a mask, skin pulled tight over her skull—the result of too much plastic surgery. As the wives filed in, the hostess ushered them one by one into the kitchen and opened the counters over her sink.

"I guess it's pretty obvious I love Tupperware," she said, grinning, painfully it seemed, showing off her perfect teeth along with five shelves of labeled containers brimming with Quaker Oats, white chocolate chips, sugar. "There's not much I don't have," she said.

The guests sat on her floral divan, side by side, as the hostess wheeled out a demonstration for them. She pushed the lid of a clear plastic bowl down, then pulled up the side and let her audience listen to the burp. "Completely airtight," she said.

At one end of the living room, she'd set out a silver tray of Brie, strawberries, grapes, and water biscuits. On the other, there was a basket filled with crudités, including three colors of bell pepper. But no one touched the food. Indeed, it was never offered. Instead, she gave each of the women a huge brandy snifter, then filled it again and again with white wine.

By the end of the evening, they were sloshed, throwing their arms around each other on the couch, flushed, snorting with laughter. The hostess stayed sober, but led the guests in a few songs. "Let Me Call You Sweetheart," "Old Man River," and a round of "Row Row Row Your Boat." Then, they took out their checkbooks and bought Tupperware, carrying it out into the snow to their cars, stumbling and giggling.

My mother came home from that Tupperware party— the only one she was ever invited to, as far as I know— happier than she had ever been.

"You're drunk!" my father said, and my mother put a white plastic bowl on her head. She danced barefoot on the living room carpet for him.

He seemed pleased, too.

He liked the plastic items she'd picked out, and didn't ask how much they cost.

Then, my mother wore the plastic bowl on her head upstairs, and came into my bedroom.

I might have been three or four years old, dreaming in an airtight container of sleep. What could I have dreamed back then—milk, snow, sugar? What could I have known?

She knelt at the side of my bed, kissed my cheek, and I woke, rubbed my eyes, looked up at her dreamily.

The hall light shone in my eyes.

There was a halo in her hair.

It must have been that Tupperware bowl on her head.

THE DAY BEFORE MY MOTHER VANISHED, HER CANARY DIED.

"You have to take it back to the pet shop," I'd said that night. We could hear its stifled weeping from the basement all the way upstairs. "Something's wrong with that bird."

But my mother just stood in the doorway of the bathroom, a toothbrush poised near her mouth, wearing a silvery nightgown, and looked at me.

She said, "I can't."

"What do you mean you can't?"

"They offered me a guarantee, and I didn't take it. They said they'd have to mark the bird if I might want to bring it back. I didn't want them to mark the bird."

Her hair was pulled up. I could see creases around her eyes like that canary's feet, as if it had left its footprints behind on her face. She seemed more nervous than usual, and started to brush her teeth hard, running water, foaming at the mouth. From the bedroom, I could hear my father fart—loud, abandoned, like a man with nothing to lose. When she heard that, my mother threw her toothbrush down, put a hand on each side of the sink, and shook her head. "Jesus H. Christ," she said, leaning into it, as if something were finally about to snap.

The next morning I got out the canary care book my mother had bought with the bird, but never read. It was full of startling facts—

I didn't know, for instance, that canaries have no teeth. That the gizzard of a canary is full of gravel, which, instead of teeth, grinds the seed it eats.

Reading that, I tried to imagine my guts full of gravel—the terrible sound of my own gizzard grinding every night in the dark while I tried to sleep. Perhaps I'd tuck my head under my wing, too, not to hear it. Or maybe I'd sing, horribly, louder and louder every day. Maybe I'd look down at my own gray shit like a splattered skirt around me, and want to fly away.

Then I read the part that explained how disreputable bird dealers will try to sell you a female canary instead of a male. The female never sings, the book said. She'll tuck her head under her wing all day. *Be sure to get a guarantee.* A bird who does not sing, who keeps her head tucked under her wing all day, is not a well-bred bird *and will only bring you grief.*

Of course, my mother's bird sang, but its song *was* grief.

The next afternoon, when I went to the basement to feed it, the bird was dead at the bottom of her cage, wings wrapped around the silky change purse of her body, face-down—a terrible cherub, or a diseased angel's handkerchief fallen out of heaven, full of coughed-up blood and phlegm. Something an angel had sobbed into for weeks.

My mother put it carefully in a shoe box and threw it into the trash.

"It wasn't a male," I said when she came back from the garage without the box. "They ripped you off."

My mother had a look on her face I didn't recognize, and she fixed me with it.

The next day, she was gone.

THE DETECTIVE'S CONDOMINIUM IS ONLY TEN MILES FROM his office. Freedom Crest is the name of the complex it belongs to, a coil of apartments and condominiums with a small black pond in the middle—the heart of freedom, unbeating, iced over, and deep.

Detective Scieziesciez opens his garage from far away with the automatic opener on his sun visor. "That's my unit," he says, pointing to the one with cedar shingles and no lights on, except in the garage, the door rising to expose it.

It's the home of a bachelor. Leather sofa, coffee cup in the sink, the smell of carpet and charcoal. There's a wallet-size photo of a little girl magneted to the refrigerator, and a crude painting of an orchid with "To Daddy" scrawled in pencil under it. The little girl is a tiny, feminine version of Detective Scieziesciez. Dark hair. Sharp features. Her expression seems canny for a child.

"I'd offer you a beer, sweetheart, but I guess you're not of age."

He's taken his coat off and hung it in the closet, and now he's draping his tie across the back of a chair at the kitchen table. Just as I imagined, he's wearing a shoulder holster, which he slips down his arm. Out of it, he takes a stubby gun. It looks heavy, professional, and the deep blue steel of the barrel is dazzling. I feel a little queasy, thrilled, light-headed seeing it in his hand. The only thing like it I've ever seen is the hunting rifle my father keeps locked up in the basement, and this is nothing like that, nothing like that at all. This is something a man hides next to his ribs, something he'd use to kill a person, not a jackrabbit, with.

Detective Scieziesciez empties bullets into his hands, and they're thick and gold. A handful of very big and dangerous bees.

"I'd take one anyway," I say.

He smiles out of one corner of his mouth, and says, "That's my girl," complimenting my spunkiness as if it's a quality he's grown familiar with, although we have met only once, for perhaps five minutes, before today. He opens the refrigerator and takes out two bottles of Heineken and flips the caps off them with an opener, hands me mine.

"Well, for Christ's sake, you still have your coat on. Let me take it for you." The detective comes around behind me and slips my coat down my shoulders.

I feel his hand graze my upper arm. The hand with the Band-Aid.

"Have a seat." He motions me toward the leather sofa. For a moment I worry that he'll put a record on the stereo—some kind of throaty jazz—and that I'll be embarrassed by it, by the television drama of it, but he doesn't. He sits down in an armchair across from the sofa, and leans back in it.

We don't say anything.

I look around his living room, which has only a few framed prints on the wall. Something with big red stripes in the middle, a black-and-white photograph of a mountain shrouded in clouds, and an orange and two apples on a cutting board with a wood-handled paring knife. There's a magazine called *The Ohio Sportsman* on his coffee table. The sportsman on the cover is posing beside a buck with dead eyes. Both of them are grinning at the camera. There's a bit of steam coming out of the sportsman's mouth, and snow on a hillside behind them.

"You seem nervous," the detective says.

I cross my legs and pull my mother's miniskirt a bit farther down my thighs, look at the green bottle in my hand, then glance back up at him. There's only one lamp on in the room, and the detective looks even darker in this light. I can see he's smiling—teasingly, maybe. His eyes are narrower than I remembered them being. I can smell him, too. On the drive here, in his black sedan, I thought I could smell his hair. It smelled like meat.

I say, "I am, I guess," and a nervous laugh catches like an airy hook inside me, somewhere between my throat and my nose.

"Now, sweetheart," he says, "you can leave any time you want. *You* wanted to seduce *me*, right?"

I nod, not looking at him.

"Well, I'm seduced. Are you sure that's what you want? I'm a big boy, you know. I don't think we're just going to second base tonight, if you know what I mean."

I look up. I say, "I know what you mean."

"You're not a virgin are you?" He's still smiling, looking at me now out of the corner of his eye.

I shake my head.

"That's good, sweetheart. So you know what's gonna happen here, then, don't you? And that's what you want to have happen?"

I say, "Yes." I can feel a weak blue vein throbbing in my neck.

"Good," he says. "I'm not in the habit of ruining little girls. You're not a little girl, are you?"

"No." My voice is very low, as though it's come out of my stomach, or out of that dead pond at the center of Freedom Crest.

"Well, you're lovely to look at, sweetheart," he says, and I cannot help but think of a sign I saw in a china shop, *Fun to hold, but if you break it, Consider it sold*, and, scrawled under that, as if it might be too poetic for customers to explicate on their own: "You break, you pay."

When I look up he's looking at me, head cocked. "I like your little haircut there. Is that what they call a page boy?"

"I don't know," I whisper, "but thanks," and push my bangs out of my eyes.

"And I like your little titties, too," he says in a different voice, a voice that fills me up with blood. He leans forward and looks hard at me. Where his shirt is unbuttoned at the neck, I see dark hair on his chest. He says, "I want to taste your little titties," and I look down at my blouse, where my face is repeated over and over again in my gold buttons—hot coins of myself. Not even for a moment does it seem wrong to be here, or do I wonder why I am.

"Maybe I should come and sit over there," the detective says, and I move over an inch to make room for him on the leather couch, which makes a naked, human sound against my suede skirt. He puts his Heineken bottle down on the coffee table. Before he kisses me, he pushes my blouse a little farther open, looks at my white bra, and says, "Yummy."

He reaches in and feels my left breast, which is small and light in his palm. He even growls a little, pressing his face into mine.

"IT WAS EASY," I TELL MICKEY. SHE'S WASHING HER HANDS at the sink in the girls' bathroom at school. On the mirror above her face, in red lipstick, someone has written "Anne Platt is fucking Mr. Fogarty." Every morning, the janitor washes it off, but by afternoon it's always back, and has been since September, scrawled in hard, loopy cursive—

I have no idea who Anne Platt is, but I've heard she's a freshman with enormous breasts. Mr. Fogarty is the assistant principal. His eyes are Aqua Velva blue, and he likes girls. Once, when I got caught smoking in the parking lot before school, I had to go to Mr. Fogarty's office, where he gave me a pamphlet about lung cancer and winked at me. "Don't get caught again," he said.

Now, whenever I pass him in the hallway, he smiles at me and lifts an invisible cigarette to his lips.

It's never seemed like much of a revelation that some freshman girl, Anne Platt, with big boobs, might be fucking Mr. Fogarty. The real mystery is the other girl, the one who must be sneaking into the girl's bathroom every single day, writing that sentence in lipstick on the mirror again and again. All that loopy, feminine fury over what? Who could sustain a passion like that for so long? She must have had to skip classes to do it: Between classes, there were too many girls at the sinks to get away with that. Was it jealousy, or outrage, or something else?

Sometimes I wondered if the writer might not be Anne Platt herself.

Mickey hands me a stick of gum in a light green wrapper. "What was easy?" she asks, bending down to tie the lace of one of her shoes. The pleats of her skirt settle around her, and she looks like a pom-pom, dropped.

"The detective," I say.

She looks up at me. The gum is so minty in my mouth as I chew it, I can hardly inhale. It's like inhaling the steam off a block of ice, too fresh.

"Oh my God," Mickey says, standing up.

I nod. I look at myself in the mirror. My face is lost inside *fucking*, as if the word is written in lipstick on my forehead. I fluff up my hair, then look back at Mickey and smile.

"You're kidding," she says.

I say, "I'm not."

"Wow, Kat." Mickey shakes her head. "I'm truly, truly impressed."

FOUR

JANUARY 1989

FOR A FEW DAYS NOW, THE WEATHER HAS BEEN WARMER, turned the snow to damp rags—ruined, dirty, christening gowns. Phil is slopping through it on the way to our house in his muddy boots, taking big, slow steps, like a cartoon character stuck in tar—exaggerated, as if the thawed ground is sucking him down. His coat looks old, plaid, and scratchy. It was probably his father's.

Since graduation last June, since he's started working at Sears full time, Phil has begun to look more and more like a boy who could be his own father. His gangliness has turned, almost imperceptibly, almost overnight, into an old man's stoop. Now, when he comes to visit me at college, driving his father's Dodge four hours north, smoking Marlboros all the way, listening to the frenzy of WKLL, then WKSS, then WZZZ—all those stations playing music that sounds like flimsy, brilliant sheets of tin being drilled together in factories all across the Midwest at once—there are ashes on his collar, and that coat smells like exhaust, pollution, a rest stop.

By the time he gets to Ann Arbor, Phil has passed through some of the dirtiest places on earth—gray weather hanging over the highway, heavy with grime, and it's settled on him, in his hair, which is too long now. The flip at his collar, too blond, the yellow-blond of a school bus. As Phil and I pass by the girls on the hall in my dormitory, they look at him sideways, as if he is a spy from another world, the world we've exited, at least for a while—the world of the suburb, the parent, the mall—or as if he might shed that dull world, walking, as if the stagnation of the place he's driven up from were a virus in his tears, in his blood.

All weekend, Phil will drink beer in my room, play heavy metal too loud on the stereo next to my bed. He'll look uncomfortable in the cafeteria with his guest ticket and a white plate of Swiss steak on a tray. He'll go to the library with me while I study, sitting slumped in a reading chair, looking at a magazine, then looking up, scanning the students with no expression on his face.

My roommate doesn't like him.

He doesn't look like a college boy.

"What does he plan to do with his life?" Cindy asks.

Cindy's from Oak Park, Michigan. Her father is an ophthalmologist. Her hair is red—deep, autumn red—and she's decorated our room with posters of Baryshnikov, arty black-and-white photographs of the dancer in tight tights, arms outstretched like a masculine bird. You can see the bulge that is his balls and penis stuffed into those tights— that stilled masculinity, that muscular dancing.

Sometimes, studying, I look up at Cindy's posters and feel a flush of blood spread across my chest.

When he came to visit the first time, Phil looked closely at those posters and said, "Gross."

"He's got to take care of his mother," I tell her.

"So?" she says, chomping gum.

Cindy plans to be a genetics counselor and wastes no time on excuses. To her, everyone's destiny can be plotted out on a graph of X's and Y's. Some of us should never have been born. She dates a graduate student from the school of natural resources, who believes our natural resources will soon run out, and twice she's tried to fix me up with his friend, Aaron, who wears hiking boots and bandannas and spends his summers on a research boat off the northern shore of Lake Michigan, looking at muddy weeds under a microscope.

At first, we didn't hit it off, but on our second date,

just before I left for Christmas break, we drank a lot of warm, imported beer, and when Aaron kissed me good night, our tongues flitted wet and silky into each other like the coincidence of fish in a large, murky lake, accidentally touching.

I know he is the kind of date I should have. Not Theo Sciezesciez. Not Phil. Someone to make plans for the future with.

But the future bores me.

I imagine following it like a leaf into traffic.

I imagine eating it like a heart made of oatmeal.

"Someone called for you," she says from her bed in the dark one night when I get back to the room with Phil.

"Who was it?" I ask.

Phil stands in the doorway, waiting: We try to wait until Cindy's gone to sleep before coming back to the room to sleep. Phil takes the edge of the bed near the wall, farthest from Cindy. In the mornings, when we wake up, she's usually gone.

"It was *Shh-shh-shh*," she says, sounding groggy but annoyed. I've told Cindy about the detective, about my relationship with him, and also told her that I don't want Phil to know. Later, he and I will have a small, dry argument about it. She's aware of this.

"He sure calls a lot for someone who hasn't managed to do one thing about your mother's case in two and a half years, don't you think?" Phil will say, but he'll drop it as soon as I get defensive, as if he knows there's more to this than he wants to know.

The day after the night Aaron and I kissed, Phil came to pick me up and bring me home.

As soon as I got home, I called the detective. "I've got a cold beer waiting for you in the fridge Saturday night, sweetheart," he said, as he always says.

What was I doing, I wondered, with all these men? I thought how, if you removed their hearts from their bodies and set all three out on a table, you couldn't tell one from the other. So what was I doing, suddenly, with all three of them at once?

Now, Phil's crossing the shallow daffodil ditch between us: Nothing even close to blooming there. Maybe this year it won't. Maybe Phil's finally trudged through them so much, Mrs. Lefkowsky's bulbs have given up, gotten the word, heard the ruthless boots above them, and decided to stay underground.

My breath on the bedroom window makes a humid, quickly evaporating kiss out of Phil, just a circle on the glass where the imprint of my lips has kissed away his face.

MY FATHER SEEMED PROUD AND RELIEVED THE DAY HE AND his girlfriend, May, drove me up to college.

"Good-bye, good-bye!" he waved from the front seat of his new car—a black Cadillac with leather seats. Riding to Ann Arbor in it had felt like hanging in the air from long elastic bands. Sixty miles an hour's worth of world rushed by, and it was nothing but a liquid blur.

I imagine my father bought the Cadillac to impress May, who is exactly like her name—a petite container of spring that could explode any moment in a frenzy of petals and baby birds, screaming. She might have giggled uncontrollably on her first ride in my father's new Cadillac.

May's a good girlfriend for my father, I like her—

who could not like May?—but being in her presence for more than an hour makes me feel ditzy, agitated, a bit slaphappy, and very tired. As we converse pleasantly, I feel my voice rise higher and higher in pitch to match hers, as if we've both been breathing helium, gasping at weightless white balloons as my father sits in slim-lipped silence between us, seeming pleased.

At one time, May was married to a textbook salesperson like herself. "But he was always depressed," she said. "He never wanted to *do* anything." Her hair is ash-blonde and bobbed above her ears. Permed tightly, it stands up all over her head, as if, at the beauty parlor, she got zapped with a cattle prod and it made her perkier, but nervous.

She's a lot younger than my father—only thirty-four—but seems maternal, in a childlike way, and eager to pick up where my mother left off. The day they left me at the University of Michigan, she had a lot of advice about college, about boys, about life. After we'd hauled my boxes to the room I would be living in (Cindy wasn't there yet, and it was blank faced—all linoleum, just two thin mattresses on metal frames, two battered desks, and a sink that echoed *boing boing* as it dripped), May said, "Don't take drugs. But if you do, make sure you know what you're taking. Someone slipped me some angel dust in college, and I've never been the same."

It explained a lot.

I imagined May in college—studious, sober, and unsentimental—before the angel dust incident, during which she'd sprouted wings, burst into frenetic flapping, been launched into the sky like a divine bottle rocket, and glimpsed the face of God—pure sweetness and sparkling light, like a lungful of air freshener on a cool spring day—before settling back to earth, altered forever.

"Good-bye!" my father said and waved. In his new Cadillac, they buoyed away.

The first few weeks at college, I thought things had changed—that, leaving Garden Heights, leaving my frilly bedroom and my mother's stiff armchairs, her lipsticks still lined up on the bathroom counter where she'd left them, that *I'd* finally left my *mother*, rather than the other way around.

But then the dreams began again—my mother in a white coffin, my mother in a snowstorm at the morgue. Or I'd dream I was walking with Phil across the icy Rite Aid parking lot, watching my feet, then see her face float up under my boot. In one dream, May came to me in my bedroom back in Ohio and said she'd found my mother in the cardboard container of a TV dinner. In another, Detective Scieziesciez looked up from between my legs, where he was giving me a dream orgasm—the kind you never reach, the kind you wake up still wanting—and said, "By the way, your mother called my office. She's in a bank-deposit box in another town."

In the middle of every dream, I'd wake up screaming, and Cindy would be standing over me in her boyfriend's SAVE THE WHALES T-shirt, biting her nails. "Jesus, Katrina"—she likes to call me that because it's more ethnic, more interesting than Kat—"What's wrong with you?" she'd ask. In the morning, she'd look at me carefully, as if I might crack right down the middle like a plaster statue, badly cast, and step out of my body.

It touched me when she said, "I'm worried about you."

We'd only shared a room for a few weeks, but we were friends.

She said, "Does your therapist know about these dreams?"

I haven't seen Dr. Phaler since August, when she wished me well at college, shook my hand, told me to call her when I came home for Christmas break if I wanted an appointment, if I felt I needed help. I never told her about Detective Scieziesciez because there never seemed to be a way to bring it up, and I stopped telling her about my dreams long ago, when she made it clear she didn't think they had anything to offer. "Dreams don't necessarily *mean* anything, Kat. We all have very strange dreams."

And I wondered then, why? Why do we all have strange dreams? Why doesn't sleep just switch off our brains like a light?

Instead, all over Garden Heights at night, bankers and lawyers and housewives are attending orgies, talking to the dead, flying over their own houses naked, wearing wings, and then it's forgotten, everything is normal, and the plumber calls to say he'll be a little late.

How is it we manage to get out of bed in the morning, face each other, organize our ordinary days, knowing where we've come from, and where we'll be going again?

A few days after my father and May dropped me off in Ann Arbor, Detective Scieziesciez called and asked me if he could come up, meet me at a Sheraton Inn, spend the night—he had some business in Lansing, and I was in between—and I said yes, although my first classes were the next day, and I was nervous. I wanted to appear bright-eyed and eager to my professors, my fellow students, but I also wanted to spend the night with Detective Scieziesciez, never actually having slept a whole night with a man.

A few times, Phil and I had fallen asleep on the couch together, and I'd stayed at the detective's condo once until five o'clock in the morning, but I wanted a whole night, dusk to dawn, in bed with a man, like a boat ride from one end of a black pond to the other.

"Hi," he said when he answered the door to his hotel room.

I'd taken a cab to the Sheraton after he called me in my dorm room and said he'd just checked in. The cab-driver was a young woman with a long blonde ponytail. She had two armloads of silver bracelets, and as she steered they made wiry music. "Ann Arbor's great," she said. "You'll like it here." The cab smelled faintly of marijuana. "A guy tried to cut my throat last week"—she turned to show me a wound on her neck, just below her ear.

"Hi, sweetheart," Detective Scieziesciez said. He was wearing a blue-striped shirt, button-down, with the sleeves, as always, rolled up, USMC on his forearm, and a pair of neatly pressed green slacks. His hair was combed—but all that thick, dark hair never really looked under control, just as the beard he tried to shave never looked shaved. In the last six months, I'd learned about his body hair, too. How it became damp and matted with sweat while we had sex. There were a few gray hairs mixed in with the black ones on his chest, but other than that he had the body of a very young man. Muscled arms and stomach. His legs were as solid as wood. He ran seven miles a day, and lifted weights for hours every night. "Got to keep myself fit for the young girls," he said, teasing me.

I knew he had other girlfriends—one even younger than I—and two ex-wives who lived nearby, one of whom brought their daughter over to his condo to visit him every Sunday, but who also came by alone occasionally on Friday nights, to have sex.

I wasn't jealous. I had Phil, after all, myself. And what

I'd wanted from the detective all along was this undaunted virility. Sometimes, when he crawled on top of my body in bed, I closed my eyes and saw a corral full of bulls tearing up the grass, snorting, glistening black in the bright sun.

It was Labor Day weekend, and I was wearing a white sundress with spaghetti straps, white sandals. I wore pink blush, and only a little lipstick. "I like it that you're so tiny," he said once, his big hands on my naked rib cage. "I feel like I could snap you in half," and he squeezed my torso hard, "but I won't," and then he laughed.

That night, beside the detective in his hotel room double bed, I couldn't sleep. I was hungry, and uncomfortable. He'd fallen asleep in the middle of the bed, and I had just enough room to lie beside him with his arm thrown informally over my bare chest, oppressively heavy, as though a log had rolled onto my body and was pinning me down with its casual weight.

I could hear other rooms under and above us. The squeaking of bedsprings. Water running. A telephone rang, sounding hysterical, but far away. The light-blocking curtains on the window did not block out the light from the parking lot outside, and there were shadows draped across the detective in thick ropes. His sleep seemed to get deeper and deeper, like a train gaining momentum as it cut through a landscape of long grass. His hair sparkled darkly. During sex, he'd sweat a lot, and it seemed he also did this in his sleep.

Then he started to snore. Quietly at first. But, like his sleep, it deepened. It sounded like a dictionary being violently paged in his chest. *A* through *Z*. I closed my eyes and tried to sleep. I thought of sheep wandering slowly around in fields, and tried to count a few of them before I slipped from the thought into a dream. But then I saw a butcher, holding, in one of his white gloves, a piece of meat across the glass counter. He was showing the piece of meat to my mother.

"Lamb chop," he said.

Was I dreaming, or just thinking?

And then Detective Scieziesciez began to groan.

Low, difficult groaning.

He didn't move, stayed heavy where he'd fallen asleep, but the groans began to stretch out longer and longer, and grow louder. My heart started to beat harder, and I wished I had my clothes on. I felt cold, naked, afraid, wide awake. When he began to shout—words, though the words were unintelligible, the rise and fall of sentence structure, muffled—I shook him by the shoulder. "Theo," I said, "Wake up. You're dreaming."

But when he didn't wake, and did not stop shouting, I reached up and turned the bedside light on, and shouted, "Theo! Theo! Theo!" I could see that his face was twisted, a look of torment, or sexual pleasure. Then his eyes popped open, and he looked up at me.

I was standing now at the side of the bed with my arms crossed over my bare breasts.

"What's up?" he asked, rolling onto his back, rubbing his eyes.

"You were having a nightmare," I said, and I realized there was a note of panic in it. "You were shouting and groaning and . . ."

"Well, come back to bed, sweetheart. I'm sorry I woke you." He was smiling. He scooted over to make room for me, and he patted the spot beside him in the bed. It was damp.

The sheets felt too warm and tangled when I pulled them over me again. I was shaking. "What were you dreaming?" I asked in a whisper. I wanted to talk. I did not want to turn the light back off.

"I don't know," he said, propping himself up on his

elbow to look at me. He pushed my bangs away from my face and traced my cheekbone with his finger. "I have bad dreams. Violence."

"Always?"

"A lot."

"What are they about?"

"Mmmm." He thought. "Things I saw. When I was a regular cop, I saw a lot of things."

"Like what?" I wanted to know.

"Mmmm." This time he thought longer. "I saw a man shoot his own kid in the head."

I didn't say anything.

"You want to hear this?"

I nodded, but didn't look at him.

"I saw a guy bleed to death real slow in the back of a truck. He'd gotten his throat cut."

I tried to imagine it.

I imagined that slash across the man's throat like an opening in the earth. I pictured the detective looking into it. There were beetles and frogs down there. I tried to imagine whether or not Detective Scieziesciez, in this scene, would be frantically trying to help the man, or whether he just watched.

"And some much worse things. I've dug up some pretty unhappy bodies."

I thought of my mother.

I thought of her lying next to my father in the morning, listening to him snore.

"One thing I know for certain, sweetheart, from being a cop, is that the safer you think this world is, the less safe it gets."

"YOU MEAN YOUR MOTHER JUST *DISAPPEARED?*" CINDY SAID, her mouth open in big surprise. We were drinking Riunite Royal Raspberry wine in our dorm room. She was cross-legged on her bed. I was sitting on the floor, leaning up against mine, legs tucked tightly to my chest. Exams were over. We were wearing nightgowns, like a little girls' party, except that we were getting plastered.

"Yeah." I nodded, and took another slug of the wine, which was the color of blood when they've just taken it from your arm—the deep velvet red that fills the vial. It was lush, warm, and gory in a clear plastic cup, tasting like a late harvest—the fruit overripe and juicy, sloshing on the vines, sloppy and heavy in the trees: I imagined the palms of the fruit pickers' hands stained permanently red. The wine was going to my head.

Our dorm room seemed slippery around us, and Cindy's face, under her crimson hair, was huge and pale in the bright overhead light. Her expression was fixed with surprise. I said, "Poof! Here today, gone tomorrow," and heard myself slur.

"Wow," Cindy said, and paused a long time. She was thinking with her plastic glass raised in one hand. It was the color of her hair, and I remembered seeing, once, a mosquito drowned in a glass of my mother's burgundy at a picnic, an end-of-season party for my father's losing golf league. My mother had reached into the glass, fished the limp, winged thing out with her fingernails, and flicked it in my father's direction when he wasn't looking.

I imagined, in all that liquid red, that the mosquito

had died of joy, thinking it had finally found the heart of God itself, and stung it.

"Where *is* she?" Cindy asked.

"Who knows?" I said. "I don't."

"She has to be *somewhere*," Cindy said.

"Does she?" I said, spilling wine on my flannel nightgown. "Maybe she doesn't. Maybe she's *nowhere*." I smiled.

But Cindy looked serious, and sad.

THIS YEAR THE GRANDMOTHERS DIDN'T COME FOR Christmas. Zeena hadn't called for months, and when she called on Christmas Eve, she didn't bother to ask about my mother. When I told her my father had a girlfriend, she sighed and said, "Life goes on, Kat. You can be sure your mother has gone on with hers," and there was an edge of prejudice in it like the blunter side of a knife—the kind of knife you'd use to pare an apple, nothing too sharp, but a knife nonetheless.

She said the weather in Las Vegas was bright and dry.

Marilyn sent a basket of fruit that must have weighed fifty pounds. The UPS man left it on the front steps—oranges and grapefruit and a fan of green bananas wrapped in red cellophane. When I opened the front door and saw it waiting, I thought some woman's elaborate hat must have blown off and landed there.

That basket was exactly the kind of hat one of my grandmothers might have worn—ferocious but feminine, shimmering fruit and rubies—a hat like a minor explosion, maybe an IRA bomb left in a trash can at the train station, no one killed, just a warning, just one innocent man, a bystander, left standing near it, waving his bloody hands. A slightly violent, semi-edible hat.

In the center, there was a coconut, as hard and hairy as a shrunken head. "I LOVE YOU!!!!!LOVE, MARILYN!!!!" the gift card said in an unfamiliar, feminine, florist's hand.

I weighed the coconut in my palm. When I shook it, the watery milk inside it sloshed.

May and I made Christmas dinner for my father, Phil, and Mrs. Hillman—the usual seared hunk of rare roast beef surrounded by carrots and potatoes. Rice pudding. Flour-dusted rolls that left everyone's upper lip smudged with chalk. May even molded green Jell-O into the shape of a cornucopia with little squares of canned peach and pear floating eerily in the green, like goldfish in suspended animation in a scummed and weedy bowl—dormant and adrift at the same time.

I felt bored.

I missed Cindy, and our dorm room, and the happy routine of class, study, cafeteria—all of it washed with strong coffee and diet Coke. Phil cut Mrs. Hillman's beef for her, and she chased the pieces with her fork around and around her plate, where they'd suddenly become animated as soon as she tried to catch one. My father complimented May profusely on everything she'd made before he ate it, and she batted her eyes at him like a cartoon Tweetie bird. A few times, I tried to catch Phil's gaze, but it was locked on his greasy knife.

"Merry Christmas!" May ejaculated, and we all raised my parents' wedding crystal into thin air to toast.

Toasting, I imagined us smashing that crystal so hard between us that it would explode in a shrapnel of champagne and flying glass, opening little eyes all over our faces and hands.

After dinner, Phil and his mother went home, and May and I cleared the table. She was wearing a sweater with a Christmas tree on it. There was so much yarn involved in that sweater, I couldn't help but wonder what would happen if it snagged. Would she be spun around like a spool, some kind of battery-operated ornament, as that sweater unraveled around her? Would her spinning make a sort of wind-up music—play a version of "Jingle Bells," or "Onward, Christian Soldiers?"

"Kat," May said shyly, her arms loaded down with dirty dishes. "Thank you so much for including me in your family gathering."

"Sure," I said, too fast, and shrugged.

She put the dishes down on the kitchen counter, looking serious—as serious as a woman with a corkscrew perm and dimples, wearing a Christmas tree on her chest, can look. She said, "I want to ask you a question," lowering her voice—though my father, by now, in his post-dinner ritual, had moved from the toilet upstairs to the bed, where he was dead asleep and couldn't hear us.

"Go ahead," I said. I picked up a sponge just to have something in my hand.

"Well, Kat." May cleared her throat. "You and I have never talked about your mother."

I squeezed the sponge. It felt like the sea creature it used to be—animal, and rank, dyed plastic orange to disguise it. "Not much to talk about there, I guess," I said.

May thought about that, then she said, "Your father doesn't say much either, but I can't help but have questions. Kat, do you have, you know, any theories at all about what happened?"

I pretended to think, sucking in the side of my cheek and chewing on that. "Midlife crisis," I said. "Or a boyfriend."

May nodded slowly, pensively, then asked, "But where is she?"

I said, "I do not know," pronouncing the words carefully, emphatically, as if May had already asked me this a hundred times.

"WHERE DID SHE GO?" MAY WANTS TO KNOW. SHE'S balanced a stack of white plates precariously at the edge of the kitchen counter. Outside, the wind howls. The windows rattle in their frames like loose teeth.

"I don't know," I say, watching those dishes, waiting for them to fall. I have my hands in the kitchen sink, which is filled with soapy water, and I can see something eel-like swimming in it, near the tips of my fingers. Suddenly, its tail licks out of the suds, orange and twitching, and then it's in my hands—a live thing, tentacled. I hold on to it as tightly as I can, and push it back under the soapy water, press it down to the bottom of the sink. I don't want May to see it, but she's watching me closely with a worried look on her face.

IN THE MIDDLE OF THE NIGHT, I WAKE UP DRENCHED—THE salty heat beneath my sheets and blankets like a fire that's been doused with sweat. Physical. Sexual. Oceanic. My legs are tangled in those sheets and in my flannel nightgown. Everything is wet.

I get out of bed, rocking, as if I've just stepped off a

ship, and I feel my way in the dark to the bathroom for aspirin. From his bedroom, I can hear my father snoring, a human foghorn, a warning snoring across an ocean. I remember how my mother hated that snoring. How, over breakfast nearly every morning, she'd complain. How once she'd even said, a serious look on her face, as if she'd been thinking about it a long, long time, for two decades maybe, "I just want to put the pillow over your father's mouth some nights, and let him suffocate."

I flip the light switch, and the row of bright round bulbs above the medicine chest glows all at once, blinding me. My eyes ache with fever, too wide and dry for their sockets, as if they might bulge right out of my head like those small bulbs themselves.

The bathroom still smells like my mother, disinfected. Her perfume, too.

But, for the first time, I notice that the little mirrored tray where she kept her bottles and lipsticks and wands of this or that—mascara, shadow, concealer—is no longer on the counter beside the sink. The guest towel with her initials, *EC*, embossed in blue, no longer lies beside the other, the one with his, *BC*.

I open the medicine chest to look for the Bayer, and in it I see a prescription bottle that wasn't there when I left for college. I take it down and read the label:

"Elavil. Refills (3). TAKE I EACH A.M. FOR MI-GRAINE."

The prescription is in May's real name: Maybel M. Engberg.

I put the bottle of pills back on the shelf and laugh a little to myself, thinking of May sleeping, regularly, with my father, keeping her A.M. prescription here because she's here in the A.M.—trying to sweep the evidence of my mother away, the perfume bottles, the monogrammed towel. Why? Is she jealous? Does she think, perhaps, my mother might come back? And what if she does? Had May thought about what she'd do then? What if my mother comes home some night, turns her key in the lock, and climbs the stairs to her bedroom, where May snores beside my father—tight curls arrayed on my mother's pillow, bony feet poking out beneath the lace of a white nightgown, maybe touching with affection the cold, hairy ankle of my father?

May's sweet mouth would be gaping open in the dark. Asbestos, lunar ash, and whatever leftover dust of my mother still floated over that side of the bed would film May's pink tongue. I imagine my mother hooting at that, and I laugh a little, too—a hushed, painful laugh—imagining May and my father trying to hide the evidence of their nights together before I came home for vacation. I imagine my father hurrying around the house, packing up May's things, which would have begun to accumulate, as these things do—her women's magazines and earrings, her extra pair of reading glasses—stuffing them under the bed, maybe. Checking the house one last time for the details that might give them away.

And here, plain as day: May's Elavil, waiting.

Sneaky, I think, and picture my father in a bathrobe, wearing slippers, tiptoeing through a garden of white tulips, lopping their heads off with a golf club. *Whop* is the noise they make as he lops them.

I sleep like someone thrown into the river with weights chained around her when I go back to bed.

But I wake up sicker. Pure fever. The bedroom is humid with it—sweat diffused with furnace dust. My sickness smells like a jungle: close, and overgrown. My head and limbs ache with the kind of dull physical pain that seems to come from far away. Not stabbing or stinging pain. Radiating pain. As dull as longing.

My father sits on the edge of my bed, and, with the thermometer in my mouth, I can't talk, and he says nothing. The silence embarrasses me. It's embarrassing to be his grown daughter, home on vacation from college, with a child's fever. And I think he can probably smell me—bodily, intimate, the smell of something private, swabbed. I remember the look on his face when he found me with Phil in my bed. It was as if someone had thrown a cup of milk in his face, that chalky look of surprise. I saw my father over Phil's shoulder. My legs were spread. Phil had a hand on one of my breasts—

Seeing that look on my father's face, the word *copulation* came to mind.

Something clinical and as humorless as botany, as cauliflower.

I can't remember my father attending to any of the minor illnesses of my childhood. Croup. Flu. Strep.

It had always been my mother who'd held the glass thermometer up to the light, reading its flimsy red vein of rising blood. When my temperature was normal, she always seemed delighted, as though she'd caught me in a lie. "Get ready for school," she'd say, slipping the thermometer back into its vinyl sleeve.

But when it was high, she'd ministrate—cool compresses, clean sheets, ginger ale, tepid tea. She'd bring me a cup of chicken broth to sip, and it would have a waxy half heart of fat floating on the top.

That pale yellow of a chicken was like forbearance, boiled down to oily water.

After a minute, my father takes the thermometer out of my mouth. "A hundred and three," he says, and his eyes get wide. He's wearing a suit, ready for the office, and each one of his silver hairs is combed into place. He thinks, and then he says, "I'll stay home from work, but I think we should call May."

I laugh, but stop short. My throat hurts—little beestings all around my tonsils, and the epiglottis feels swollen, like a fleshy fishhook in my throat. I say, "Dad, it's okay with me if May sleeps over while I'm home. I'm old enough to deal with that, you know."

"What do you mean?" he asks, and his impression of an innocent, accused, is good. His black eyebrows are raised in a startled line.

"I saw her prescription in the medicine cabinet. 'Take one each A.M.' So I assume *it's* here because *she's* here each A.M. And that's okay with me."

"Oh, that," he says. "Oh, well, yes, sometimes she spends the night. But . . ."

"Dad, it's really okay." I try to sit up. He hurries to fluff the pillows behind me.

"Let me get you some juice," he says, "and then I'll call May to see what you do about a fever like this."

I SPEND THE NEXT MORNING AND AFTERNOON IN BED, sipping orange juice, which stings bitterly going down. But my father brings me glass after glass and, after it's swallowed, it feels good. It cools me.

I fall asleep for a few hours, and the fever drags me in and out of a dream in which I'm trapped in a burning building, standing outside an elevator under a sign that reads IN CASE OF FIRE USE STAIRS.

But somehow I know there *are* no stairs, so I stand there, flames inching down the hallway toward me as I try to decide whether to take the elevator up or down—not knowing which button to push to get there because they're side by side, and marked in Braille. Since I can't read Braille, I'm afraid to make a mistake, afraid I'll make the right decision, the one that will save my life—whether to go up or down—but push the wrong button. As the flames move inexorably toward me in a bright parade—a wall of vivid oxygen melting everything as they come—finally, out of desperation, I close my eyes and feel the raised bumps.

Amazingly, I can read them with my fingers.

One of the buttons is marked Now, and one is marked Later.

I pause for a moment, then press Now, and the doors open immediately, but the elevator is filled with smoke. In the center of it is my mother. She steps out of the elevator calmly, not particularly surprised to see me, and says, "You're getting warmer," with an amused look on her face.

MAY'S ALREADY LEAVING WHEN I WAKE UP. SHE MUST HAVE come over while I was asleep. I hear them at the front door. "No," my father says, "I just don't think it's right with her here."

"But if Kat says it's okay, I don't see—"

"I don't care what Kat says." He whispers loudly, sounding irritated.

I sit up—rubber-limbed and warm, like a baby who's been left by accident all afternoon in a very warm bath. "Dad," I yell from the top of the stairs when I get there. "I insist that May stay over. May," I shout, though my voice scrapes my throat, "I want you to stay."

"I—" my father says. I can see his face at the foot of the stairs, turned up to me, a big dog about to beg.

"Dad," I say, teasing him, "be good. May stays. I'm going back to bed."

May giggles. "Well, Brock, that settles that, I guess."

TODAY SHE'S WEARING GREEN. DEEP, CHRISTMAS GREEN. Evergreen. She smiles as she ushers me into her office.

"So," Dr. Phaler says. "How are you? How have things been?"

"Fine," I say. "College has gone well. I got three A's and a B. It was a good semester. I've been sick since Christmas, though. Fever. Chills."

She nods. "The flu," she diagnoses. "Everyone's got it." Dr. Phaler smiles then with her lips closed. "I assume," she says, opening her mouth in a tiny bullet hole before going on, "that you haven't heard from your mother, or you'd have mentioned it when you called for the appointment."

"No," I say, and it hangs in the air. My own lips are pursed now like hers, as if my face is a reflection of Dr. Phaler's. "Detective *Shh-shh-shh* called a few days ago to say they'd closed the case, for whatever it's worth."

It wasn't exactly true, but also wasn't a lie. Detective Sciez-iesciez *had* told me they were closing my mother's case, but he told me about it in the water bed in his condominium. The water in the mattress was warm, and when I moved I felt embraced by its formlessness, its bodiless fluid.

We were talking about dreams again, because again he'd dozed off beside me after sex, and again I'd had to wake him out of his shouting.

So I told him about mine:

The dreams of my mother calling to me from the coat closet in our living room, and when I opened the door, there she was, lace veil over her pale face, maybe two great wings wrapped around her body. Shivering. And then she'd disappear.

He seemed to think about that for a long time.

"Why didn't you tell me about these dreams before?"

"When?" I asked. "Why?"

"Sometimes dreams make a difference," he said seriously. "Sometimes people know something they don't know they know."

"What do you mean?"

He thought. He said, "I had a case once where a two-year-old had been missing for days, had just wandered away from a picnic at a park. It was assumed to be a kidnapping, but the mother kept dreaming the baby was in the back of a truck being driven away while she watched. Sometimes she'd even get a glimpse of the license plate, and finally she woke up one morning and was able to write the state and number of the license plate down.

"We tracked the U-Haul down in Minnesota—it had been rented by a college student, he'd driven through Ohio on his way to California—and the kid was in the back. He'd crawled into it at the park while the student was changing a flat tire and eating a sandwich—crawled way far in the back. The guy threw the flat in the back, slammed it shut, and didn't have any reason to open it again until we got there."

I felt nauseated.

The water bed.

I could smell it—salty and old in the plastic mattress. Chlorine. Swamp. Small and soggy sweaters.

I sat up and swung my legs off the bed, and looked at my bony, cold feet on the beige of the detective's bedroom rug. I thought of that little boy turned to milk and rags in the bed of a truck. All because Detective Scieziesciez wasn't smart enough to find him before he'd sobbed and gasped and sucked himself to death.

But, I thought, the point of this story, as the detective told it, was how smart he was. What a good detective.

I kept staring, hard, at my feet, and I thought of the letters we used to get from his office, the ones with my mother's name misspelled. I remembered him knocking so hard and efficiently on our front door that first time, months already since my mother had disappeared, and how he'd stumbled, bumbling, when I opened it. I remembered, suddenly, Officer McCarthy, that cop who'd visited our fifth-grade class to scare us about drugs, and pictured him wearing a dunce's cap, sitting in the corner of a classroom as a lot of little children snickered.

Another big, dumb, muscled man with a gun.

I will never come here again, I thought, and curled my toes into the carpet, and my feet became as blunt as clubs. "How could she have known that?" I asked, "How could she have dreamt that?"

My voice was brittle. Maybe I was shouting. The detective sounded defensive when he answered, and he got out of bed, pulling his boxer shorts up. The water bed gulped.

"Obviously, she saw that truck at the park and some part of her registered that the kid had crawled in there. She was too hysterical to consciously understand that, so it came to her in dreams."

"Oh," I said. "Then what's up with *my* dreams, Detective? Where's my mother?"

Detective Scieziesciez zipped up his jeans, and looked down at me. He looked a bit confused. He began to flex the bicep of one arm and feel it, knead it with his fingers, as if to remind himself that he was strong. Then he sighed. "Well, do you really want my opinion?"

I pulled the sheet around me, hiding my nakedness. "Of *course*," I said. "Since the very beginning we've been asking for your professional opinion." I raised one of my eyebrows ironically as I said *professional*.

He began to look angry and worried, a man having to defend himself for the first time in his life. "Well," he said, "in that case, in my opinion, your mother is dead."

There was whining in my lungs, but it had nothing to do with me. It sounded like knives being sharpened on ice. I knew he was going to say this. I could tell he would want to hurt me. "Why?" I was interrogating *him* now.

"Because an extensive and very well-handled search for her has been taking place for the last three years, and she has not been found."

I could see blood rising up his neck, and I knew suddenly, clearly, that there had been no search at all, that he was lying, or incompetent, or both.

" '*Extensive*' and '*well-handled*'?" I asked. "You never even spelled my mother's name right in your letters. That photo you used on the flyers was so blurry, she could have been anyone. You never looked *anywhere* for my mother. You never even looked in our house!"

He pulled his leather belt quickly through the belt loops around his waist, and it made a windy sigh.

"First of all," he said, "my secretary types up the letters. The spelling errors are hers. Second, your father provided the photo we used, and he said it was the best he could do. And third, we can't search a house without a search warrant, and we can't get a search warrant without some reason to conduct a search. I had to assume that if your mother was in the house, you'd have been able to find her yourself. She wouldn't exactly be *missing* if she was in the house."

"Okay, Detective. Where is she?"

"Well, you yourself indicated that she was probably having an affair, which was confirmed by that woman, that Mrs. Blindman, next door—"

"Mrs. *Hill*man."

"Whatever. The blind lady. She said your mother had a boyfriend."

"What would Mrs. Hillman know? *How* would Mrs. Hillman know *anything* about my mother?"

"She lives next door." He smirked when he said this.

"But she can't *see*." I felt afraid that I might cry. I took a deep, painful breath. "Besides, wouldn't that just make it even more likely that she was off somewhere with this *boy*friend"—the sarcasm caught like a sob in my throat—"not dead?"—and so did *dead*.

"Well," he said, pausing, staring at the bedroom wall, narrowing his eyes. It looked as if he were reading his lines off a cue card he couldn't quite see. "Well," he said again, "several people interviewed told us that your father is a jealous and impulsive man."

The detective's stomach looked like stone covered with skin. He was buttoning up his white shirt.

"Who? Who was interviewed? Who said my father was '*jealous* 'and '*impulsive*?' My father, if you couldn't tell this for yourself when you interviewed him, is one of the dullest men on the planet. Obviously, whoever was interviewed never met him."

I imagined my father then, wearing a clown suit, having a pie thrown in his face by Detective Scieziesciez. There was pie in my father's eyes, and he was wiping it out, and the image made me grimace with protective rage.

"That's not what their former neighbors at the Ramblewood apartment complex had to say. Bob and Mattie Freelander. They said your father suspected your mother had a thing for Bob Freelander, and that your father set a trash can on fire and tossed it onto their patio."

"*What? What?*" I gasped. I was standing now, fastening my bra behind me as quickly as I could. "Who are these people? My parents lived in that apartment *two decades* ago."

The detective shrugged. "So? A man's nature doesn't change in two decades."

"A '*man's nature*.'" I started to laugh, but it sounded

like an animal heaving something up. *"My father hasn't got a 'nature.'"*

Detective Scieziesciez regained his composure as I lost mine. He sat on the edge of his water bed looking at me, distant and concerned, though there were already dark rings of sweat under his arms, and he'd just put on his shirt. I couldn't find my panties. I had to get on my knees.

"Kat," he said to me at his feet, "any man is capable of anything. Trust me. I know. Any man could kill his wife if he caught her with another man—a younger man, a richer man. Men kill. *I* know."

"Oh," I huffed at him. My panties were under his nightstand. I sat on the floor to pull them on. "You don't know shit," I said "If my father's such a dangerous character, why the hell didn't you arrest him, *Detective*?"

"You can't arrest someone just because he's *capable* of murder." He stared blankly at my panties. They were lacy and white. "There wasn't any evidence. And he passed a lie detector test. Your father's a cool guy, *if* my suspicions are correct. He knew what he was doing when he got rid of her. In my professional opinion, your father caught your mother in the act, killed her, and dumped her. Maybe the Chagrin River. It was January. She'd have slipped right under the ice. By spring, she'd have washed to Lake Erie. We won't be finding your mother. Hence," he shrugged, "this case is closed."

"But," I tell Dr. Phaler, "that's not what I wanted to talk about. I don't really expect to hear from my mother, ever again. I've accepted that."

"Still," Dr. Phaler says, shaking her head, "that must be a fairly hard thing to accept."

"Yes," I say, waving it away with my hand, feeling annoyed. She's leading me, like a horse. I will not drink. "But my problem right now is Phil. I want to break up with him. I don't know how."

Dr. Phaler runs her tongue over her top teeth. I notice that her glasses aren't hanging from the usual chain around her neck and that her eyes, like her outfit, are green. Didn't they used to be blue? She's gotten contacts, I guess. "Tell me more."

"Well, he's been so good to me. But we've changed. Or, I have. I want to date another guy. I met this other guy." An image of Aaron flashes, then, across the ceiling tiles when I look up—red bandanna around his neck, playing a guitar. I'm not sure, but I imagine Aaron plays the guitar, and badly. I imagine one day he'll own a big, smelly dog—a black Labrador, and he'll take it with him in his truck when he moves to Oregon.

Then I imagine Detective Scieziesciez holding a gun to Aaron's head, forcing him to open the back of that truck.

"Do you have to break up with Phil to date someone else?"

I think about that. "Well. It doesn't seem fair—"

"Has Phil treated *you* fairly?"

"What do you mean?"

"Well. Have you and Phil started kissing again? Or having sex? Is he making any plans for his future?"

"His mother—" I start to say.

Dr. Phaler waves now, and now she looks impatient, dismissive. "With or without his mother."

"No." I look at my hands.

"And has he ever come up with any satisfactory explanations for why that is?"

"Why what?" I ask. "You mean, kissing? I told you before, he says he doesn't see any reason to kiss."

"*Any reason to kiss?*" Dr. Phaler laughs out loud. "Who needs a reason to kiss?"

"You're right," I say, nodding. "But he's been so good. You know. He was there for me when my mother disappeared." She's looking at my neck. Maybe she's biting her tongue. The silence feels, when I swallow, like the white of an egg, or sperm, on the back of my throat.

Then she says, carefully, "Kat, have you ever considered that he might have been there for you when your mother disappeared because he felt guilty?"

"About what?" I've shouted it. I touch my throat. I'm surprised at how loud my voice has become, and I lower it. "What would Phil have to feel guilty about?"

"What do you think?" She says it calmly, without accusation. "Don't you have *any* clues?" There's an empty look on her face. A ceiling tile. It's as if the Dr. Phaler I said good-bye to last August has been replaced by a fresh, more determined Dr. Phaler—a Dr. Phaler committed to scraping the ice off her windshield with an ink pen. All business. Ready to go. Chip, chip, chip. Jaw set in some direction I'm not sure I want to go.

"No," I say. "But that's not why I'm here."

"I know," she says. "But I think it's something you need to consider. You need to consider why Phil might have stuck around all this time, despite the fact that he doesn't even love you enough to kiss you."

I see my hands in my lap as if from far away, and they are the hands of a stranger, shaking. Perhaps I sound angry when I say, "Maybe you should tell me what *you* think. Obviously, you think something."

"Well, Kat, you've told me quite a lot about your mother's behavior just before she left. Don't you think Phil might have had something to do with that?"

"What do you mean? *What* did I tell you? All I said was that I thought they were flirting—that *she* was flirting with *him*. Why should he feel guilty about that?"

But I can tell Dr. Phaler's done. Her arms have settled on her armrests, roosting, and her mouth is closed again. She nods. My hour's up.

Where did it go?

I'm not done.

"Do you think there's something I don't know? Are you saying you think there was something between my mother and Phil? Why didn't you say anything until now?"

Am I hysterical?

Is this what hysteria is? I picture a can of trash with wings landing on my shoulder in flames, and hear my voice coming out of a narrow hole, a rabbit hole.

I've shrunk, I think, looking at Dr. Phaler, who is too far away, now, to see.

I am a pinprick, a little piece of who I was. My whole face could fit on a postage stamp.

Dr. Phaler stops nodding. She seems to be thinking. I can tell by her voice that she hasn't noticed how tiny I've become—a miniature of myself in her new, green eyes. She says, "I don't know. But if you want my opinion, there's no reason to feel guilty about breaking up with Phil."

When I get back out to the car—my mother's station wagon—I realize I'm holding a handkerchief with the initials *MP* in my fist—in cursive, black, in a corner of the white square trimmed with bric-a-brac. I have no idea how it got in my hand.

I take it back and leave it draped like a veil over the doorknob of Maya Phaler's office.

PHIL STOOPS TO TAKE OFF HIS BOOTS. IT'S THE FIRST WEEK of January, but the neighbors across the street still have their electric nativity set plugged in. They leave it on all day and night and, in the afternoon, there's a weak and artificial light rising from baby Jesus, as if he's swaddled in glare, and the Virgin Mary sheds dreary bandages of blue into the cold fog. I shut the door behind him.

"Hi," he says, a little surly, a little shy. He has thin white lines around his eyes—I've never noticed those before—where the sun must not shine. The rest of his face has a winter tan, a wind tan, a reddish burn just under the skin. It makes his hair look even blonder, oddly blond.

"Hi," I say.

"You sound stuffed up," he says.

"I've been sick," I say.

I haven't seen Phil for a few days, not since I went to visit him at Sears, where we had an argument in the break room in front of another salesman. It was Saturday, and Phil had been "working the floor" as he calls it, which means sneaking up on unshaven husbands as they look at the prices on power saws, lawn tractors, dehumidifiers.

The department Phil works in is metal gray. The shelves shine with buffed light and, from floor to ceiling, are filled with the kind of items you might find in a junkyard, or dumped at the side of the road, left in the woods. Wrench sets, claw hammers, hoses, rubber mats to throw on the floor of your car, levelers, flashlights, dolly straps, fireproof safety boxes. You could imagine a grown man in bed beside his wife, a stocking cap on his head—and, above him, in the cartoon bubble that reveals his dreams, a floating menagerie of those items from Sears.

In the bubble above his wife's sleeping head, there would just be z's.

I had been standing behind a shelf, among the hand appliances—the planers, strippers, sprayers, drills—when I heard Phil, on the other side, say to someone, "This is the best random-orbit palm-grip sander money can buy," and I'd laughed out loud.

Phil sold it to the man, who was wearing an orange

hunter's vest and jeans that sagged down over his hips so that, when he leaned over the counter to sign his credit card receipt, I could see the two mounds of the man's buttocks, and the sad crack between them.

I felt sorry for that man, who kept looking at his palm-grip sander over and over again as Phil rang it up, as though he knew, somewhere in his heart, having done this so many times before in his forty-nine years as a consumer, that he was making a terrible mistake. The palm-grip sander with its random orbit would not turn out to be what he'd wanted, or needed, but he would own it now for the rest of his life. It would hang above his workbench in the basement as another painful reminder of his gullibility, poor judgment, while the waste around him accumulated like rain in old tires, or rusty lengths of pipe in the countryside.

Where would it finally go, I wondered, looking at the overstocked shelves at Sears—all this junk?

Where *does* it go?

For instance, those tires that are always wearing away, going bald on the highway—where is that rubber when it's no longer on those tires? Does it fade into the atmosphere—gaseous, a breath of rubbery air inhaled, exhaled? Or does it wrap the road in snakeskin like a jacket? Weren't we driving, every day, over and over our own shed rubber?

Still, Ohio is crammed with rubber factories—Goodrich, Diamond, Industrial Rubber Inc.—making more and more. Where does it go? Those eraser shavings—ten tons of that must be worn away every year in elementary schools all over America. Those children in their rubber-soled shoes should be knee-deep in that pink ash by now. We *all* should be—

But we aren't.

All this stuff, I thought, looking at it, rubbed away,

worn away—friction turning our things to weather and air. Where does it go?

It *has* to go *somewhere*.

The man left with his palm-grip sander in a gray plastic sack that said SEARS in maroon letters, and Phil, who had been smiling and standing up straight in his striped tie and white shirt, sagged, then glared at me. "What's so funny?" he asked.

I stopped smiling. "Well, Phil. Doesn't it strike you as just a *little* silly: 'This is the best random-orbit palm-grip sander money can buy?' " I imitated him, a slow baritone. "Just a bit melodramatic, or something?"

"Sorry to be so ridiculous," he said and turned his back to me. "I can take a break now, if you want to have lunch. If you're not too clever to have lunch with an ass-hole like me."

"Phil," I said, following him into the break room. "I'm sorry. I completely forgot that you don't have a sense of humor anymore."

He turned around fast.

Behind him, a canteen vending machine whirred, warm, its miniature cans of ravioli and SpaghettiOs waiting. I hadn't meant to sound so mean. He looked like he'd been slapped.

"Just get out of here," he said, and a salesman at the break room table looked up from his *Sports Illustrated* with a noodle hanging off his lower lip. Phil made a shooing motion with his hand. "Just go."

I left.

The automatic doors that led from Sears back to the parking lot hesitated before they opened, and when I walked through them, they tried to close on me, then stopped themselves short before jarring all the way open to let me pass.

"Let's go upstairs," I say to Phil now.

"No," he says. "Let's just sit in the living room if your dad's not home." His feet in their wool socks move nervously over the carpet—nervous, toothless animals. He sits in my father's armchair in the living room, and I sit across from him on the couch.

"Look," I say. "We both know this isn't working out."

"No," he shakes his head. "It's not. You're too smart for me now, college girl."

I sigh. This will be harder than I'd hoped it would be, harder than Dr. Phaler would have had me believe. "That's not it," I say. "There's been something wrong a lot longer than that."

Phil looks like a lifeguard out of work for the winter—wind-tanned, but his hair is turning darker around the roots. For the first time I notice he must be trying to grow a mustache, and I imagine Phil with his bristling, hardware-salesman mustache. The knees of his jeans have begun to wear away, and I try to feel the compassion I used to feel. "Poor little boy with a blind mother," I remember my mother whispering as she watched him load Mrs. Hillman into a car to drive her to a doctor's appointment, folding her into the passenger seat in her big winter coat, stuffing her in.

But Phil seems weak to me. I used to imagine a little satin heart with his name embroidered on it in my chest. A pincushion. A souvenir. The kind of thing you might buy in a gift shop, something that says "Las Vegas" or "Be Mine." But now, there's a cold, white stone in there instead—as if, during an apathetic kiss, something dead from inside him had slipped into my mouth, and I'd swallowed it whole.

It didn't used to be like this.

I could still remember dancing with him in the gym:

How young we'd been! A sudsy bloodbath of energy. Fat, in my pink dress, I was a sad valentine made by a child, made out of cotton balls, dime-store doilies, and paste— sentimental, pathetic, a little desperate, but sincere. And Phil was stooped but not yet bent, jerking to the music in his blue tux. Whatever burdens he already had, they did not seem permanent.

And all those sweaty nights on the couch, his kisses like blurred stars all up and down my neck. I was still fat. Together we were wading into a tepid lake. Carefully. The mud was soft and as loose as flesh.

But that was a long time ago.

"It's over," I say. "You'd better leave."

"Okay," he says, standing up. He doesn't seem surprised in the least. "But there's something you should know."

"What?" I ask. Whatever it is, I think, I won't care. Phil looks dilapidated, shrugging on his plaid coat.

"Your father knows perfectly well where your mother is," he says.

"Excuse me?" Sarcastic.

"You heard me." He's putting his boots on. Reptilian. They're army green, prehistoric-looking. The slick boots of a swamp dinosaur. Waterproof. Fireproof. "He's keeping her up his sleeve."

I sigh and roll my eyes. Typical Phil, I think—mangling his clichés up to the bitter end. I picture my father with my mother slipped into his shirt on a stage in a kind of vaudeville show—aping in a top hat, the whole audience guffawing at the absurdity of this joke.

"What do you mean?" I ask, impatient.

"Ask him," Phil says, opening the front door, stepping through it. "Don't ask me."

I SIT IN THE LIVING ROOM IN ONE OF THE GREEN-WINGED chairs for a long time. My father has gone to work. Outside, a plow scrapes through the streets, throwing snow to the side of the road, and the snow sounds soft, physical, a solid wave lapping at the curb, tossed out of the way. I picture a cow standing on railroad tracks, the huge machine of a train on the way, and the muffled, vulnerable sound of that cow in its path.

And then I remember the sound of her voice, which was as much a part of my mother as her body, but disconnected from her, hovering around and above her, as voices do. She had a soft voice, though it was often edged with sarcasm, judgment, displeasure. I picture vowels, wrapped in light, rising from her in clouds, as if something tangible could be made out of sound. I think, If the phone rang now, if I picked it up, and my mother spoke to me through the receiver, would it mean she existed any more physically than she does already, living in my memory, in her silence?

"Have fun," she'd said, here, in the living room, as I left through the front door with Phil on the night of the Winter Formal four years ago.

"Have fun." I'd handed her the corsage box he'd brought with him when he'd come to pick me up. The rose that was in it, surrounded by its baby's breath, was pinned above my breast, and the box was empty. When my mother took it out of my hands, I could see it was lighter than she'd thought it would be, and cold. Phil must have kept it in his refrigerator at home. As I left for my first date, in the living room my mother was still holding that cold emptiness in her hand.

Fun was the last thing she wanted me to have.

I go to the kitchen, and take a carton of milk out of the refrigerator.

MISSING, it says on the back, and there's a grainy photo of a fat little girl right under the box where the calories are counted. On the side, there's a boy in a striped shirt. HAVE YOU SEEN ME? he's asking with a big lost smile on his face.

I pour myself a glass of milk and take a long sip of it before I again remember that two-year-old in the back of some college boy's truck, his skin softened, turned to liquid.

The milk is cool and vaguely sour when I swallow it, gag, spit it into the sink.

When I look up, my father's standing in the doorway of the kitchen. He hasn't taken his boots off. There's snow falling in soggy fractions onto the floor, and a trail of it melts behind him.

MICKEY'S ALREADY DRUNK WHEN SHE COMES OVER WITH two bottles of champagne in a brown grocery sack. My father lets her in, and I hear him upstairs introducing May—the sound of May's singsong sweetness, and my father's formal discomfort. Beth and I are in the basement, waiting, sitting on the floor, leaning up against the vinyl sofa. My mother's birdcage hangs over Beth's head. We've never taken it down—shining, brightly empty.

"The bird has flown," Beth says, looking up at it.

When I called Mickey and Beth that afternoon to tell them I'd finally broken up with Phil, they both insisted on coming over to celebrate. Over the phone, Beth said, "God rest his soul."

Mickey's wearing a leather jacket, and when I hug her, I smell smoke and animal skin. She kisses Beth's cheek as she slips her jacket off—casual, magnanimous, European. I haven't seen her since August. Since then, her hair has grown longer, been styled into wisps around her jaw. She's wearing a black turtleneck, and makeup—burgundy lipstick, black eye shadow, a pale-beige base. With the turtleneck, the makeup, and the hair, she looks less scarred than I've ever seen her, and no longer a cheerleader. Mickey looks like a painter now, or a poet. The energy that once secured her spot on the varsity squad despite her unloveliness—that energy has turned overnight into a kind of serious intensity that is, finally, darkly beautiful.

She smokes clove cigarettes.

She's dating a music major—bassoon.

It sounds like a swan, she says. A very sexual instrument. Once, in his dorm room, she let him tie her to the bed. She's asked him for a pair of handcuffs for her birthday. They might even move to New York. All this she told me when I called to tell her that Phil and I were a dead issue.

Tomorrow, Mickey goes back to Madison. The day after that, Beth leaves for Bloomington. And the next day, my dad and May will drive me to Ann Arbor. We've decided to spend tonight like old times, getting drunk in the basement and smoking and talking together in our old cocoon, while, above us, my father stomps around in slippers.

"Jesus," Mickey says. "I don't know about you two, but I can't stand to be back here. It's like purgatory. Purgatory, Ohio. Haven't we done enough time here? I can't fucking wait to get back to school." She sits across from us on the basement floor, at the edge of the carpet remnant, lights up a clove cigarette, and the smell of the smoke as it fills the basement and our noses is like a garden fire. A burning bush. The smell of a flower arrangement, torched, or the Christmas lights, shorted, igniting the whole tree in a smoldering moment. Mickey's not wearing a bra under her black turtleneck, and her breasts look autonomous and big.

Beth is wearing old jeans and a flannel shirt. She's gained more weight since she went away. She likes to study, she says, but she hasn't made any friends. A few times, on weekend nights, alone in her dorm room with her roommate gone, she'd thought about what it would be like to be dead, how easy it would be to buy a gun—a small one, with a mother-of-pearl handle. There were pawnshops all over town. She'd considered how hard or easy it might be to hold that gun to your temple, count to ten, just as an experiment, to see how close you were willing to get to death, what *ten* felt like when you said it: a teaspoon of lead on your tongue, or a brass key to the door you were ready to step through into the colored light, the jagged surprise of a geode when you smashed it, all crystal and amethyst and pretty points inside.

But she wasn't sure she wanted to die, at least not yet.

"Get me the fuck out of here," Mickey says.

"I know what you mean," Beth says. "My mother told me to clean my room this morning, and I wanted to bludgeon her with a feather duster."

Mickey pops the plastic cork on the first bottle of cheap champagne, and there's the wind of foam and pressure and the seething of trapped, effervescent space unleashed. Then she pours a little for each of us into my parents' wedding glasses.

"So, congrats, Kat." Mickey raises the glass. "Phil's out of the picture at last."

"At last," I say. "God." I shake my head, feigning sadness. "What a mess that ended up being."

"Or," Beth says, "as Phil would say, 'What a vicious triangle.' "

The champagne chokes me with tartness and bubbles.

"God," Beth says, swallowing. "What a dolt he was."

"What I liked," Mickey says, "was the look he got on his face when he was rubbing a couple Big Ideas together," and she makes the look—a stern, fatherly frown.

"Not a guy with a fancy interior, that's for sure." Beth smirks.

"Here's to Phil," Mickey toasts. "May he never again loaf in vain."

"May he never love in Spain." Beth raises her glass, too.

My palm is flat against my chest, gasping with laughter, eyes watering, thinking of Phil—how he wore his sleeve on his heart. I remember reaching under him, between his legs, while we fucked, touching his balls. In my hands, they felt loose, and invertebrate, and at my mercy, and I'd thought of a marble Madonna I'd seen once at the Toledo Art Museum. She was holding the world in the palm of her hand, and seemed pleased. There was a thin, mysterious smile on her lips, as if she knew how much power she had.

But then I remember the look on Phil's face as he shrugged his father's coat on, how much taller than me he seemed, how that expression was smug, as though we'd just finished playing a game—a dangerous game, a game played with pieces of broken glass and aluminum bats—and he'd won.

I drink. I say, "But there was a parting shot."

"I hope it wasn't a shock in the dark," Beth says.

"Or a shark in the pot," Mickey says.

I'm laughing again. I feel better. Finally, I say, "He

told me he thinks my father is keeping my mother up his sleeve."

Mickey nods at Beth, then at me, in mock reflection. "Sounds reasonable," she says.

"A bird up the sleeve is worth two bushes at least," Beth says. "Or so they say."

We laugh harder, and for a long time. Then, when the laughter's faded, I lower my voice. I say, "No, really, you guys, he says my father knows where my mother is."

"Hmmm." Mickey strikes a match and lights another cigarette, and her tone changes. "Does that surprise you?" she asks, looking at the tip of her cigarette to see if it's lit. She drags on it, then says, "Personally, I've always wondered about that."

Beth nods, looking at me seriously.

"Really?" I stand up quickly with the unopened bottle of champagne in my hand. "Why haven't you ever said anything?"

Beth looks at Mickey, who looks at Beth, and then at me. She says, "I think I did. Once. Right after she left, Kat. But you didn't seem to want to hear it." She continues, "I remember asking you if you thought maybe your dad had something to hide, if maybe he knew something you didn't and wasn't saying, and you just blew it off. You said he was too transparent to hide anything. You said he'd taken a lie detector test, and they'd decided your father lacked the ability to lie."

I stand there with the bottle, and they look up at me uneasily in the silence. Finally, Mickey pours herself some more champagne. She says, "I've been drinking all week. I just *hate* Garden Heights."

"Maybe I should put this bottle in the freezer," I say.

I feel groggy, and confused, as if I've just hit my head hard on something soft. I hold the champagne bottle like a skinned chicken, by the neck, and go into the unfinished part of the basement, and flip the light switch.

One bare bulb blazes from the ceiling, a terrible brightness.

I feel tired, blinded by it, as if I've been sleepwalking and have just woken up with a searchlight in my face. I can hear Mickey and Beth laughing in the other room, my father and May talking in a muffled singsong upstairs, but I can also hear myself breathing, and the breath sounds as palpable as wings, or water, in my lungs.

I head for the back of the basement, past the washer and dryer, across the drain hole, into the shadows, to the freezer. I can hear it purring, a contented vibration that hums through the whole white length of it, humming into the cement floor, into the earth under that. My father's piles of old newspapers, bundled, are tied up tightly, efficiently, with twine on top of them. Years' and years' worth of old news. He must have planned to take them to the Board of Education's annual paper drive one of these years, and forgot, and keeps forgetting, as the piles grow higher.

I set the bottle of champagne on the floor.

The bundles are heavy, and yellowed, and the twine cuts into my fingers when I start heaving them off of the freezer. They make a lifeless *whoomf* as they hit the cement, and the headlines seem strange, hopelessly innocent and outdated, even a little insane, staring up at me.

U.S. DOWNS TWO LIBYAN FIGHTERS. SURROGATE MOTHER MARY BETH WHITEHEAD SOBS IN COURT. Ronald Reagan's colon cancer. George Bush looking weary, jogging in Kennebunkport in the rain. And, at the very bottom, a bundle that must have been there since the year my mother disappeared. A photograph of the Challenger making its last, crazy zigzag through the sky as it loses its challenge with space.

When all the bundles are off, I put the palm of my hand on top of the freezer, and feel the warm motor of it running. It must get hot, working so hard to keep the things inside it cold. I haven't opened it since before my mother left, and when I try to lift the lid, I can't. It's as though something's holding it closed from inside, or as if a huge, invisible weight is resting on it.

I try harder, my fingers under the white rubber lip, straining. I can feel the frost on my knuckles, but I can't lift it, and I quit trying. I pick the bottle of champagne up, start back to the other room, turn the light off as I leave.

"The freezer won't open," I say, still holding the bottle by the neck.

"Forget it," Mickey says. She lifts her empty glass for more champagne. "Let's just crack it now."

I sit back down on the floor, handing it over to Mickey, who struggles with the cork as Beth and I look on, holding our breath, waiting for the bright, foaming shot that doesn't come. Instead, I hear my father at the top of the stairs. "What's going on?" he shouts down to us. "What are you doing down there?"

Mickey puts the bottle between her knees and grinds out her clove cigarette in the ashtray, looking surprised.

"Drinking champagne, Dad. We're just talking and drinking champagne," I call up to him. "Why?"

"I want those girls to go home," he says. His voice sounds strained. "Right now."

Beth frowns at me, puzzled. I shrug. I stand up and head toward the stairs to ask him what's wrong, but when I get to the foot of them, he's already gone. I hear him stomp across the kitchen, through the living room, where I hear him say something in an angry tone to May, and she replies, also unintelligibly, in a high, apologetic whine. Then I hear them head together up the stairs.

"Jeez," Mickey says, slipping her leather coat back on. "What do you suppose that was all about?"

LYING IN BED, I THINK OF MRS. HILLMAN WANDERING through her house in the perpetual dark, arms outstretched, feeling her way to the bathroom, the sink, the sofa, the refrigerator.

Born blind, what if, one morning, she opened her eyes and could see?

I imagine Phil finding Mrs. Hillman in her bed that morning when she doesn't get up, doesn't shuffle down to the kitchen for breakfast. Phil finding his mother lying on her back in her own bed, eyes bulged out of her head, mouth a gaping hole of surprise—

She'd seen it all too fast, for the first time, and had died.

Maybe, I think, when you've waited a long time to see something, you need to find your way to it in glimpses.

A tatter of color.

A sharp triangle.

A glimpse of smudged light shining off the coffee table on a summer afternoon.

A leaf, a wing, a swaying branch, a fragment of black trunk, a brushstroke of bird's nest before the whole tree's illuminated—shrill, and undisguised, filling your empty eye with its dazzling razors and knives, an explosion of edges and circles and straight lines shivering.

Green.

Brief.

Movement.

Screaming.

You'd have to be ready for that.

THE SNOW HAS MELTED, AND THE MUD HAS COME TO LIFE: Trees and tulips, muskrats and possum are sucking up out of it with a sluggish sound, like some beast giving birth to a whole world—the sound of lactation, phlegm, and swimming, while in the muck something swampy and furred licks its blind young with a long sloppy tongue.

In the garden, there are hundreds—thousands—of baby snakes, sexual and twisting, suckling at wet nests of broken eggs and the fresh shoots of new leaves in the branches over my head, still damp and curled into fetal fists. I'm barefoot, looking up at the sky, which has begun to shed a fleshy, gray rain, then down at those snakes, eating their own tails now, when suddenly I notice my mother.

She's under me, clawing herself slowly out of the thawing ground. Naked, writhing, she's being born, sitting up, and it's her hair I notice first, strung with the sludge of January, melting. Then she wipes the mud from her eyes, looks up at me, and says, "I'm glad to be alive."

When I wake up, May, wearing a white nightgown, is standing in the dark of my bedroom doorway. I realize I'm drenched in sweat, and naked. In my sleep, I've pulled my flannel nightgown up over my head and thrown it to the floor. The sheets and blankets have been stomped down to the end of the bed—shed. May's mouth is open wide, looking at me, and I am screaming and screaming and screaming.

IN THE MORNING I HEAR MAY TALKING TO MY FATHER IN the kitchen. She says, "Something's terribly wrong."

My father grumbles, guffaws. "She has a nightmare," he says sarcastically, "and there's '*something terribly wrong.*' Haven't you ever had a nightmare before?"

"Not like that," May says, hushed and serious. "Not like that."

"Well, I have," he says, dismissing her. "Plenty."

I hear something slam. Maybe he's pounded his fist on the kitchen table. "I told you not to sleep over with Kat here. I told you."

May starts to whine. "I don't see why you're so upset. I'm just expressing concern about your daughter."

He's shouting now. "My daughter does not need your concern. You are not Kat's mother."

"You're right," May says, resigned. I hear hangers in the coat closet. She's getting her coat. She says, "I have to go to work. Call me tonight if you still want me to drive Kat to Ann Arbor with you tomorrow. Otherwise, I won't bother you."

"Good," my father grunts.

"Oh," May says.

"What?" he says.

"Nothing," she says, and I hear the front door slam behind her.

"DID YOU ASK YOUR DAD WHAT THE FREAK-OUT WAS all about the other night?" Beth asks over the phone. She's leaving for Bloomington this afternoon. Mickey left for Madison yesterday without calling to say good-bye.

"This morning he said, I kid you not, 'I won't have girls smoking in my basement,' " I tell her.

"What?" Beth laughs. "We've been smoking in that basement for five fucking years, and he knows it."

"I know," I say. "I told him that, but he just walked out the front door, got in the car, and drove off to work."

"Weird," Beth says, drawing the word out.

"Well, it doesn't matter," I say. "I'll be back at school tomorrow. I can smoke myself into a stupor if I want to. I can smoke my way to oblivion and back."

"Yeah," Beth says. "But not with me and Mickey. Not in your very own basement. Not in Garden Heights, Ohio." She sounds sad, like someone who doesn't want to be where she is, but knows she'll never be back.

"Well, all third-rate things must come to an end."

"Or," she says, sounding cheerful again, "as Phil would say, 'All's swell that ends swell.' "

When she hangs up, I keep the receiver at my ear for a long time, listening to the dial tone until the recorded voice of the operator comes on and says, "Please hang up and try your call again."

That voice sounds far away, echoing across the miles,

like a woman who has been living at the end of a tunnel for a long time.

Then there's silence.

"Beth?" I say into the phone, but she's gone.

I PACK MY CLOTHES AND SHOES AND BOOKS. IT'S AFTERNOON. I leave for Ann Arbor in the morning.

This time, I'm taking more things back with me than I brought home. I'm taking things I thought I'd leave: my photo albums, my jewelry box, my summer shorts, a straw hat I bought long ago with a big plastic sunflower on the brim—a hat I wouldn't be caught dead in now.

I'm taking the pink dress, three sizes too large, that I wore to the winter formal with Phil. I've been saving it for years, like a memory, and I don't want to leave it here.

When the suitcase is full, I get another out of the guest room, then I go to my parents' room and open my mother's closet.

It is entirely empty.

I look at the emptiness a long time, and try to see into it. I try to see past it. The way Mrs. Hillman looks into the vast whiteness in front of her all day, stepping carefully into the snow on the other side of herself, sniffing the air as she goes.

But the longer I stare, the more empty the emptiness becomes, and brighter. It's as if I've opened a closet into pure space—flat, but cavernous, and shiny—as if, if I stepped into it, I could fall into the future forever. I stare, and don't breathe, and step closer, looking harder, until I think I recognize a face in there. A woman emerging. A grown woman with her mouth open, wearing a white scarf, a halo of light in her hair.

I gasp, leaning in. "Mom?" I say before I realize she is only my reflection. There's a mirror in the back of my mother's closet, and nothing else.

When I hear my father behind me, I turn around—

I had no idea he was home. He's wearing a suit. His eyes are dark and narrow. Why isn't he at work?

"What are you looking for?" he asks.

"Nothing," I say.

"Well," he says, "you found it."

He goes back down the stairs, and the door closes behind him with a dry, sucking sound.

WHEN MY FATHER COMES HOME AGAIN, IT'S FIVE P.M. HE doesn't say hello. I stay upstairs. We don't have dinner together. May doesn't come over. My father falls asleep in one of the green chairs in the living room, and I come downstairs to find him in it. He looks as stiff as a crossing guard, snoring. I go back upstairs.

It was a gray afternoon, but as the sun goes down tonight it lights up the horizon, dipping below the sky's steel wool in an angry frown. From my bedroom window I watch it sink into the earth, making a black silhouette of Phil and Mrs. Hillman's house. I think of them inside it, seeing and unseeing, sitting down to dinner.

A boyfriend. I remember. She told Detective Sciez-iesciez that my mother had a boyfriend.

And I remember calling them the Saturday after my mother disappeared, how Mrs. Hillman said, "I'm sorry to hear your mother left, but, no, I didn't see anything unusual at your house yesterday."

She'd been gone only one day. I said to Mrs. Hillman, "I'm sure she'll be back soon, but we're going to the police station this afternoon to make a report."

There was silence on the other end of the phone.

Then Mrs. Hillman said, "Did you get the cookies I sent to school yesterday with Phil?"

I thought: Cookies? There was a paper plate of fuzzy yellow stars covered with plastic wrap on the kitchen counter. I thought they were left over from Christmas. But they did have the look of cookies made by the blind, I realized then. How could Mrs. Hillman know what a star looked like, or what color one was?

"Yes," I said. "Thank you. Yes."

"Here's Phil," Mrs. Hillman said, handing over the phone.

"Hello?" He sounded strange, and farther away than next door.

I said, "Why weren't you in school yesterday?" before I remembered Mrs. Hillman saying she'd sent him to school with the cookies that were in our kitchen now. Apparently, she didn't know he wasn't there.

"I went to the mall," he said. "I bought you a present." He was whispering, and he sounded fatigued, maybe a little resentful. "It's our anniversary," he said. "Didn't you remember?"

"Oh," I said. "Sure." But it threw me. Phil and I hadn't been romantic for quite a while, and I hadn't remembered our anniversary or bought him a present, and I couldn't imagine what he could have bought me. A Barbie doll wearing a pink dress like the one I'd worn to the Winter Formal on our first date came to mind. She had synthetic hair and pins stuck into her chest.

"That's nice," I said, trying to sound grateful. "I'd

have called sooner, but we were trying not to tie up the phone. My mother's gone."

"She'll be back," Phil said flatly, but he was still whispering.

"How did these cookies get here?" I was looking at them. I'd wandered into the kitchen with the phone receiver at my ear. The cookies were smudged under the plastic wrap. Blurred. Stars. They did not look edible. The one in the center was cracked in half.

"I brought them over to your mother," he said. "Yesterday. I brought them over and dropped them off," he said. "Then I went to the mall to buy your present."

I heard my father coming down the stairs. "Kat," he said, "get off the phone right now. We have to keep the line open."

I watch their house from my bedroom window until the sun sets, seeming to breathe fire for a while in the bare January trees before it settles its flaming sword into the west edge of Garden Heights.

And I remember the present he gave me, the one he said he'd gone to the mall that day to buy. It was a tape. *The Top 15 Dance Hits of 1985*. At the time, I'd thought it was either the most or least thoughtful present he could have come up with. Either he'd considered long and hard what to buy me, spent all day wandering through the mall, worrying, and then he'd remembered our first date, all that dancing, the disc jockey hired by the high school to play the theme from *Miami Vice* over and over in the dark—or, it had been the quickest and easiest thing to reach, hundreds of them on display near the cash register, waiting.

"I hope you like that," Phil said as I turned it over in my hand. He hadn't wrapped it. When I looked up at him, he shrugged.

But I didn't like it. I started to listen to it one day on

the tape player in my mother's station wagon, but I'd seen the MTV videos for every one of the songs, and those videos were what I saw—models dancing in bikinis, slippery images of thin women moving their hips in nervous splices on the television set in our living room—not Phil. Not me. And the music seemed slippery, celluloid, as well. All the instruments electronic, all the voices filtered through a computer. It made me feel nostalgic already for 1985, which had only been over for a few weeks, listening to Glenn Frey sing "The Heat Is On," and it made me wonder how simple, how naive, how faded and unrecognizable we'd seem to ourselves in *fifty* years, looking back at those videos, considering the songs we'd listened to and liked. Our lost, bad taste in clothes and music betraying our innocence. Our celebrities dead in accidents we had no idea they'd have. Our current events turned into trivia questions: What was "New Wave"? What British rock band was "Walking on Sunshine" in the summer of 1985?

We'd keep looking back at ourselves in those shoes with that hair and shake our heads at how goofy we were, how sure we were of something that turned out to be nothing.

Then, the sky turns black, but clear, and now the stars blink on, one by one by one, as if God is moving through the halls of heaven flipping the light switches as he goes.

I stand at the window a long time in a white nightgown, and the night gets blacker, until I can no longer see outside, until the window is just a reflection of my bedroom, of my white gown. The furnace blows warm air into the room, and there is the smell of crayons melting, or the smell of my mother's perfume in early summer, sun shining on her bare arms as she drove me home from school.

The smell of hummingbirds and butterflies baking in a dish at a low temperature for a long time.

Eau-de-Vie.

The numbers on my clock radio flip themselves forward without hesitation, with the determination of mechanical things.

When 11:59 flips into 12:00, it's a new day.

1:00 A.M.

2:00 A.M.

3:00 A.M.

4:00 A.M.

5:00 A.M.

6:00 A.M.

When I hear the first winter birds of morning start to sing, I start down the stairs again.

"KAT."

I hear her.

I can't see the sun coming up—my eyes are closed—but I feel it breaking out of the ground, tearing the east edge of the earth to pieces, rising under the suburb, rocking our house—big fists breaking through the basement floor, shuddering through the concrete, a great volcanic eruption through the drain hole, lava and sparks spewing, something giving birth, or being born.

"Kat."

She's there. I finally know where. I start down the stairs, toward the sound of my name called, called in that familiar voice that has been muffled for so long—as if I'd been hearing it through a wall of flesh and blood, a body separating us, from which I've just emerged.

Now, it's like radiance calling my name, everywhere at once.

———

I follow it through the hallway to the living room, where my father's still asleep in the green-winged chair. There's something he's stayed here all night to guard, but his eyes are shut, head fallen backward, blankly facing heaven, or the ceiling, or the loosening dark above Garden Heights. His face is a mask softened by sleep. Still, out of his mouth there is a roaring, human sound, threatening and deep, as if he's kept a furnace hidden in his chest for years. I pause there, and the snoring expands.

It thunders through the living room. It shakes the walls. A hundred hooves. A hundred doves. It's kettle-drums, and chariots, and war, and it blows the curtains open, and through them I can see the way the lawn rolls with whiteness away from the house, rolls toward the street, snow curling back into the sky, the present rushing into the past, and I imagine Phil, barefoot, running across it, running home, running away from my father shouting, "*Go. You coward. You boy.*"

And his mother, waiting there for him. She must have known—

Soft stars exploding behind her eyes.

She must have called my father at his office.

"Mr. Connors. This is Mrs. Hillman."

"Yes? Mrs. Hillman? What—"

"Your wife has company this afternoon. I think you should go home, that you should see."

It was a Friday. He had nothing else to do.

I go to the top of the basement stairs, and stand, and listen for a long time. I listen until I hear the whole world down there. The howling dogs, and wings, and the whirring of machines, and wind, and screaming, blunt objects, the buzzing of bees, rifle shots, and a million mothers calling their children with music like rivers on fire.

I listen to it until my whole body becomes an ear. My hair. My breath. My teeth. And then I follow her voice—

her voice, which rises out of all the other noise, the voice that named me, the first voice I ever heard, the voice that called me out of her skin into this world.

Down the stairs to the basement. Past the pool table. The vinyl couch. The finished part. The canary's empty cage—just a tuft of pale molt leftover, a fistful of echo, or weather.

"Kat."

And then she's screaming me past the mute witnesses of washer and dryer, water and fire, past those appliances of silence, of politeness, and convenience, saved time— farther into the unfinished part.

Open this.

Open this.

"What?" I ask her. "What? The freezer's locked."

"But you know the combination," she says. "You've always known."

I find my way to the Coldspot and stand barefoot before it. A trunk of infinity. Stuffed with sparks and talismans and dreams. A mind made out of nothing but love, fear, space, saying my name, creating creation.

Atoms, radio noise, God, and the matter of stars, all waiting to be bathed in brilliance, to reveal their secrets in sudden, stunning light.

I try to open it. I grip the top of the freezer, lock my knees, hold my breath and strain, but it won't open.

So I get down on my knees and feel the half-inch of frost and space where I can slip my fingers into it, until I find what's holding it closed. There's a lock snapped through a hole that's been drilled in the handle, and the lock has been slipped into the freezer.

I pull it around and out, examine it in my hand— though I don't need to see it to know it's the combination lock my father used to keep on his file cabinet, the one in which he kept his magazines. 36-24-35.

It opens simply in my hand—a needle dropping into a stack of hay.

I don't move. I listen.

And then the gray matter of January begins to melt all around me. "Here's Mama," she says, and the vowels rise in two frozen zeroes above the freezer, swallow each other in midair.

How? For the rest of my life, I'll be asked *how*, and this is what I'll say:

Like any other daughter, I simply came to this darkness barefoot, and mortal, and just like her, when I heard her call my name to the silence, which wasn't silent any longer. And then—

I lifted its lid, looked inside myself, and there my mother was.